"I don't want you to touch me!" Sarah said sharply.

"Sure you don't," Brad replied.

Then, with the briefest flicker in his eyes, as if he had told himself he ought to know better, he lowered his mouth, pausing just before his lips touched hers. She could have pulled away, but she didn't. She said nothing. She didn't even breathe. His hand still nestled on her neck, he covered her mouth with his.

His lips were warm, dry from the sun and the wind, gentle. Sarah closed her eyes and absorbed everything about the kiss—the feel, the promise, the longing.

His hands shot around her waist and pulled her to him, his thumbs digging into her sides. Her body molded against his, began to loosen, relax, her shield shattering as she knew only the taste of his lips and the hardness of his big body against hers. His mouth claimed hers more fully. *Brad, Brad, where have you been all these months, all these years?*

WHAT ARE *LOVESWEPT* ROMANCES?

They are stories of true romance and touching emotion. We believe those two very important ingredients are constants in our highly sensual and very believable stories in the *LOVESWEPT* line. Our goal is to give you, the reader, stories of consistently high quality that may sometimes make you laugh, sometimes make you cry, but are always fresh and creative and contain many delightful surprises within their pages.

Most romance fans read an enormous number of books. Those they truly love, they keep. Others may be traded with friends and soon forgotten. We hope that each *LOVESWEPT* romance will be a treasure—a "keeper." We will always try to publish

*LOVE STORIES YOU'LL NEVER FORGET
BY AUTHORS YOU'LL ALWAYS REMEMBER*

The Editors

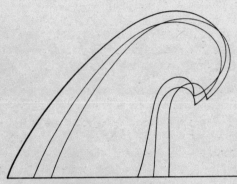

LOVESWEPT · 36

Carla Neggers

A Touch of Magic

 BANTAM BOOKS · TORONTO · NEW YORK · LONDON · SYDNEY

A TOUCH OF MAGIC

A Bantam Book / March 1984

LOVESWEPT and the wave device are trademarks of Bantam Books, Inc.

ISBN 0-553-21636-8

Published simultaneously in the United States and Canada

Bantam Books are published by Bantam Books, Inc. Its trademark, consisting of
the words ''Bantam Books'' and the portrayal of a rooster, is Registered in U.S.
Patent and Trademark Office and in other countries. Marca Registrada. Bantam
Books, Inc., 666 Fifth Avenue, New York, New York 10103.

PRINTED IN THE UNITED STATES OF AMERICA

O   0 9 8 7 6 5 4 3 2 1

One

Sarah waited on the front porch with her fingers twisted together, her teeth gritted, and rainwater dripping off the end of her nose. She hadn't felt so vulnerable in years, but there was nothing she could do about it now, not with the storm still raging, the hour approaching midnight, and her hamstrings strained far beyond their capacity. And her eyes. Her left contact lens had disappeared hours ago, and her glasses were useless in the downpour.

At last the door opened. Sarah's throat tightened, but she recovered and stepped forward with a vague smile as yet another stream of water dripped out of her hair, down her forehead, down her nose, and plopped onto the porch floor. She squinted at the blurred figure in the warm light of the entry, but with her 20–500 vision she could tell only that it was tall and male.

"Mr. Craig? I know I'm seven hours late, but I can explain."

She stopped. She had narrowed her squint so that the man's features weren't quite so fuzzy, and she could see that he didn't look like a man in his late sixties. But Bradley Craig had retired to the Catskills three years ago. He had said so in his letter.

Sarah took a step backward and wondered if in her confusion and near blindness she could possibly have stumbled onto the wrong doorstep in the middle of the night in the middle of nowhere.

"Seven hours late?" the figure asked, his voice deep, friendly, curious. "For what?"

She couldn't have made a mistake. Impossible! Third farm on Spring Road, Bradley Craig had written; it was on the right, a big white house with red shutters, and it wasn't a working farm anymore. Sarah had practically pressed her nose against the mailbox to read the name: CRAIG.

"This *is* the Craig residence, isn't it?"

"Yes."

"Well, then, I'm Sarah Blackstone."

She didn't need 20–20 vision to know he was staring at her, and he didn't need to speak for her to know that he was thinking, Sarah Blackstone? Who the hell is Sarah Blackstone?

The butler! He must be the butler, she thought. The Craigs hadn't sounded like the sort of people who would have a butler. Bradley Craig had handwritten his note on ordinary stationery, and Dorothy Craig had followed up with an invitation written on a notecard with three kittens on the front. And yet their farm was considered an estate, and it was midnight, and—

"What about that explanation, Ms. Blackstone?"

She looked at him sharply and narrowed her squint until there were three of him standing there. He was grinning! She was standing on the front porch, drenched to her briefs and bra, in not an inconsiderable amount of pain, and the man was grinning at her! Obviously he wasn't the deferential, well-bred sort of butler she was used to, but should she explain to him? Ah, where were Emily Post and Aunt Anna when she needed them?

"Mr. and Mrs. Craig are expecting me," she said politely.

"They're not here."

"Not here?"

She supposed he nodded.

"Ms. Blackstone, would you care to come in? I'm sure we can straighten this out and—"

"No, no, that's all right," she said quickly.

So what are you going to do, Blackstone, she asked herself, spend the night under a lilac bush? The man would have a dry towel and food and hot water . . . and coffee—hot black coffee! She shuddered at the thought of what she would be giving up. Surely if his intentions were unsavory he would have grabbed her by the throat by now. But where in the hell were the Craigs? "Will they be back in the morning?" she asked.

"No. They're in Ann Arbor. My sister just had a baby, a month premature."

"Oh."

That would explain everything. Sarah had been on the road for three days. The Craigs no doubt had called or written to explain their sudden change in plans, but she hadn't been home to receive their message. So all her suffering had been for nothing. She couldn't very well spend the next few days with this grinning man.

"Ms. Blackstone, please come in. This is all very amusing, but it's wet out here and—"

"I think I—" She groaned; there was just no graceful way of doing it. "Who are you?"

He laughed. "You really are fun. Brad Craig. I'm harmless. Now, won't you come in?"

"Oh—oh, then you're Bradley and Dorothy's son!"

"Mmmm."

She gave a small embarrassed laugh. "Perhaps I should towel off first. I really am dripping, as you can see."

She could feel his gaze on her lean, soaking figure and knew her wet, lightweight clothes were clinging to her. She might have just been dunked in a pond. She certainly couldn't have been any wetter. Beneath her shirt and filmy bra, her nipples were hardened from the dampness and chill.

"It's quite a storm," he said. "I'll be back in a minute."

He left the door ajar and disappeared. Sarah went limp with relief. She was sure Bradley and Dorothy Craig were decent, honest people, and their son would be the same. She had nothing to worry about.

Brad reappeared, stepped outside onto the porch, and thrust a towel at her. She groped for it blindly, but missed and had to stoop to retrieve it.

"Are you—are you blind, Ms. Blackstone?"

"No, no." She laughed again. "At least not usually. I lost one of my contacts about thirty miles ago, and my glasses are no use at all in this kind of weather. They just fog up, and I can't see worth a damn anyway."

"You lost a contact?"

She nodded and toweled herself vigorously. It was a huge towel, soft and wonderful. "My left one. I was cruising along when this giant trailer truck hit a pothole and splashed me from head to toe, and in my attempts to keep from being smeared all over the road I lost my lens. There was no way I could find it, of course, not in that mess. If it weren't for this lousy astigmatism, I could wear soft lenses. They don't fall out nearly as easily."

"I see." He sounded amused.

"It was hell," she went on. "My glasses worked for a while, but then I had nothing dry left to wipe them on and they started fogging up and getting spotted, so I just stuffed them in my pocket about ten or fifteen miles ago and blundered my way here."

She grinned, not feeling so vulnerable or nervous now, and ran the towel over her shirt and thin poplin pants. She squinted at Brad, thinking somehow that a dry face would make her see better, but of course, it didn't. He was still a blur, if a bigger and brawnier blur than she might have expected. His fuzzy figure was at least six inches taller than hers, which was saying something, since she was a willowy five nine.

"Let me see if I have this straight," he said. "You were about thirty miles from here—"

"South of here actually. I came up along the Hudson."

"Right. And a truck hit a puddle and splashed your car—"

"Not my car!" She laughed and draped the towel around her neck. "Me!"

"You?" He sounded dubious. "Just as you *happened* by, a truck *happened* to hit a pothole, which just *happened* to be full of water—"

"Dirty, muddy water. It was awful."

"Dirty water," he repeated. "And this dirty, muddy water just *happened* to splash through your window and caused you to lose your contact lens. Come, Ms. Blackstone, I've never objected to having a beautiful woman in distress drop in on me at midnight, but surely you can do better than that."

"I am not a woman in distress."

She felt his gaze on her—a doubtful, probing gaze for certain, Sarah thought. A beautiful woman in distress? She almost giggled. "And I wasn't in a car. I was on my bicycle," she said.

He didn't day a word. He just stood there, and in two seconds flat he spluttered into laughter.

"It's true, dammit!" She flung an arm out toward the end of the porch. "There, go look for yourself. A Raleigh ten-speed."

She watched his big, fuzzy body trot down the steps and trot back up again. "Well," he said, "I will say you're creative. Now, won't you come inside, Sarah?"

She tugged on the two ends of the towel and tossed her head back. What exactly was the man implying? If she had had her contacts or even her glasses, she would have given him one of her infamous penetrating looks. As it was, she could only squint and, with a sigh, follow him inside.

They weren't two steps into the entry when she bumped into a table. "You *are* blind as a bat, aren't you?" He laughed and took her by the hand. "We're going through the land of my mother's Hummel figurines. It wouldn't do to have you laying waste to the entire collection now, would it?"

Sarah shook her head. His hand was huge and callused, but dry and warm. He wasn't being forward; he was being nice. Of course, her glasses *were* right there in her pants pocket, and all she had to do was hand them to him and ask him to polish the lenses, but she thought of that only when they were halfway down a hall lined with shelves holding the Hummel ceramic figurines. Her mind kept hammering out his name: Brad Craig, Brad Craig. Where had she seen it before? Bradley Craig, Jr.? No, that wasn't it. Just Brad Craig.

He deposited her in a small bathroom off a large kitchen and told her to make herself at home. "I don't suppose there's anything dry in that pack of yours?"

"No, everything soaked through hours ago. It's rained all day."

"You've been on the road the whole damn day?"

She nodded. "Three days actually. I'm sure your parents left a message at my home, but I wasn't there to receive it."

Even without her contacts she could see his grin. He didn't believe her. "Sure, Sarah."

She wished he would call her Ms. Blackstone. Nearly everyone did these days, and the familiar way he used her name made her uneasy.

"Look, you can put on my robe if you want, and we'll wash your things in the morning. Or I can run upstairs and fish out something of my mother's."

She hadn't thought about clothes, not having

permitted her thoughts to venture beyond getting to the Craigs' house and into a hot shower. "Your robe will be fine," she said politely.

"I thought so."

He shut the door and left.

Sarah immediately dug out her glasses, rinsed them under the faucet, dried them with a tissue, and put them on. At last she could see! She scanned the bathroom: white walls, white fixtures, white towels, white tiles, rust-colored terry-cloth bathrobe of mammoth proportions hanging on the door. It was all very neat and clean, but she couldn't find any hint of why the name Brad Craig kept thumping in her brain. Still, simply being able to *see* her surroundings restored her self-confidence.

In fifteen minutes she was standing in front of the sink combing out her straight blond hair. It was a good color and made her look like a cool, Scandinavian beauty, although she didn't have a drop of Scandinavian blood in her veins. She would have liked icy blue eyes to go along with the hair, but hers were a pale green. She had a straight nose, if a bit long, and an ordinary mouth, except that it showed dimples in her cheeks when she smiled. She had never been fond of her dimples.

She slipped on the bathrobe and seemed to disappear inside of it. Maybe she'd shrunk in all that rain, she thought, laughing to herself, and wrapped the robe as tightly as she could around her and double-knotted the tie. All right, so Brad Craig was a monster. She was dry, she could see, and above all, she was Sarah Blackstone.

Nonetheless, she crept out of the bathroom and peered at him from the doorway. He was at the stove, humming to himself as he swirled a fork around in something that looked like eggs. His back was to her. She tiptoed to the table and slid onto a pine bench.

He cocked his head around at her and grinned, as if he'd been aware of her scrutiny. "Feel better?"

She jumped. So much for stealth. "Oh, yes. Much, thank you."

"Good." He turned back to the eggs.

With her corrected vision Sarah could see that Brad Craig was indeed big, but hardly overweight. He had the most awesome legs, long and thick and muscular, the thighs bulging beneath the worn fabric of his jeans, but his hips were narrow and lean. He wore a short-sleeved gray sweat shirt that revealed big, powerful arms, and his shoulders were not merely broad but developed, as strong and trim as the rest of him. And yet somehow his body radiated not just brute strength, but energy and agility. He certainly wasn't a bodybuilder type, but who was he?

Brad Craig, Brad Craig . . . dammit all, who was he?

He scooped the cast-iron pan he'd cooked the eggs in off the heat and dumped its contents onto a plate. Sarah tried not to stare as he walked to the table. Big as he was, he didn't lumber. He gave her a quick, expert once-over that irritated her because it was so frank and flattered her because it wasn't at all uncomplimentary.

"Thank you," she said. "I could have cooked myself, but I appreciate it."

He plopped the plate and fork he had used to scramble the eggs in front of her. "Toast's cooking and coffee's brewing," he said amiably. "Anything else I can get you?"

A succinct biography of Brad Craig, Sarah thought. "No, thank you. You're being very kind."

He laughed and went for the toast. "You're a riot, Sarah Blackstone. So where do you live?"

"New York."

"Jelly on your toast?" She shook her head, and he laid the two toasted slices of bread on the counter and slapped butter on them. "Pedaled all the way up here from the city, huh?"

That doubt again! Steady, Sarah, steady. "That's right."

"Legs stiff?"

"The shower helped."

"I can't see a little slip of a thing like you bicy-cling ninety miles, but it took you three days, you said?"

Sarah had been called many things in her near thirty years, but rarely—if ever—a little slip of a thing. She was lean and long-legged, but not little. "I didn't come straight here, Mr. Craig."

"No?" He seemed surprised.

"I visited friends and a few museums along the way. It really was fun until today when the rain started. I admit I wasn't prepared for an all-day torrent."

He dumped the toast on the edge of her plate, lifted one massive leg, and sat down, straddling the bench. The knee under the table was about a half-inch from Sarah's—she glanced down to check—and the other knee was no more than an inch from her derriere.

He seemed to be waiting for her to go on, so she did. "It wasn't just the rain that delayed me though. I got a late start this morning." She smiled, forget-ting about the dimples for the moment. "I stayed with some friends I hadn't seen in months, and they made me waffles and sausages for breakfast. It was wonderful! I thought I could make up the lost time, but I had problems with my legs—"

"Hamstrings?"

She nodded. "And then there were *so* many hills! Well, I could have managed, but I got a flat, and then I lost the contact—and it was just slow going. I tried to call several times, but there was no answer."

"I was out."

"I understand." But if he had answered the

phone and told her about his parents' departure, she never would have come. She tried the eggs. "Did you, uh, put something in the eggs?"

"Yeah, my mother planted some herbs, so I cut up a few and tossed them in. Why? Don't you like it?"

"Well, I think—" She sighed, the manners pounded into her head by the Blackstone women and several editions of 'Emily Post' preventing her from telling her host she thought he had put catnip in her scrambled eggs. "They're fine."

He seemed satisfied.

She tried the toast and for the first time noticed his face. It wasn't as spectacular as his body, but it was a good face, strong and friendly. His eyes were a dark, dark brown, and they were laughing at her, or everything, and were the same color as his mass of thick hair.

"I really am sorry to drop in on you unexpectedly," she said honestly. "I wouldn't have, of course, if I'd known your parents wouldn't be here." She wondered about the grandchild and hoped the baby was all right.

"Of course."

She glanced up sharply at Brad and saw that he was smothering a grin with the palm of his big hand. He didn't believe her! He thought—

Oh, good Lord, the man thought she had engineered this whole damn thing just to—to what? Get near him? Meet him? Spend the night . . .

"Oh, dear."

He placed a hand on each of his knees and leaned toward her, so close that she could feel his breath hot on her already hot cheeks. "Something wrong, Sarah?"

"Mr. Craig, I don't think you understand," she said steadily. "I wrote to your parents several weeks ago and explained to them that my ancestors had built this house in 1797 and that many were buried on the property. I asked if during my vacation this June I could come north and examine the gravestones and tour the property."

His mouth twisted—all, she was sure, that kept him from guffawing.

She ignored him. "They insisted not only that I come, but that I stay with them for as long as I wanted. They were very nice about it. I was grateful and agreed. We set up the time, and I called last week and said I would arrive around five o'clock the following Sunday evening. I may be seven hours late, but I'm here."

Brad had put his elbow on the table and was now holding up his head with his hand. He said, maddeningly, "Right."

"I know my arrival was a bit unorthodox, but when I spoke to Mr. and Mrs. Craig last week, I hadn't anticipated bicycling up. That was a decision I made more or less on the spur of the moment four days ago."

She did not tell him that she had decided that this would be her one last wild fling before she turned thirty next month, her final attempt to recapture the spirit and innocence of her youth. And she was determined to succeed. So much had happened in so few years. Had the Craigs sensed that, and was that why they had been so kind? Sarah sighed, suddenly very, very tired.

"You don't look like the kind of woman who makes decisions on the spur of the moment, Ms. Blackstone."

So it was Ms. Blackstone again. She was relieved, but when she glanced at him, she saw that he was very subtly mocking her. She remained calm. "I don't usually."

"But just this once?"

She nodded.

He grinned at her. "Don't look so worried. I'm not going to throw you out on a night like this. People have done stranger things to get to meet me, men included. You're very charming, Sarah, and very pretty, but, if you don't mind, you can sleep in the guest room."

She shoved the plate across the table, stiffened her spine and stared at him.

He laughed. "Don't look so shocked," he said amiably. "As I said, it's not that you're not good—creative at least—and I *am* tempted, but it is nearly one o'clock in the morning." If possible Sarah thought, his grin was broadening. "And a toss in the hay with me would play hell with your hamstrings."

Sarah's mouth dropped open in indignation, but she snapped it shut immediately, rose as regally as she could in the oversize robe, and glared down at him. "I don't know who the devil you are, Mr. Craig, or who you *think* you are, but I am Sarah Blackstone, president and chief executive officer of Blackstone Industries and chairman of the board of the Blackstone Foundation. I shall thank you to keep your rude remarks and outrageous, totally unfounded accusations and insinuations to yourself."

He roared with laughter. "So that's your game. Okay, if you insist. I'm Brad Craig, quarterback for the New York Novas."

Sarah would have slapped him, but she was desperately afraid to let go of the robe and thought the gesture would only make him laugh harder. Quarterback indeed! And for one of the top football teams in the country. She clenched the robe tightly, whirled around, nearly tripped, lifted the hem to her ankles, and stalked off down the hall toward the entry, where she had seen a staircase.

"Third door on your right," he called between laughs. "Don't you want your coffee?"

"No!" She didn't even turn around. "I have enough to keep me awake, thank you!"

Two

Sarah could not believe it. She was trapped in the Catskills on a stormy night with a man who liked to think he was a football player! After everything that had gone wrong that day, now *this*. She groaned and growled and slammed the guest-room door behind her. Brad Craig was big, good-looking, arrogant, conceited, and—

Oddly familiar. Was it possible he wasn't lying?

She flipped on the lightswitch and looked around the room. Its country charm instantly began working on her frayed nerves. It was just what she had hoped for: pine and oak antiques, patchwork quilts on the twin beds, cross-stitch samplers on the walls, wide floorboards. The pitter-patter of rain on the roof brought a smile to her lips and soothed her indignation.

She was Sarah Blackstone. She had survived tragedy. She was responsible for millions of dollars. She regularly had to deal with men and women who relished outwitting her. Surely she could handle one man with the effrontery to think—

No, she wouldn't remind herself of what he had said. Quickly she slipped out of the mammoth robe—he *was* big enough to be a quarterback, wasn't he?—and crawled naked into the bed nearer a paned window.

Ah, but that luscious grin . . .

She yawned, listening to the soothing pitter-patter of the rain.

And those remarkable, laughing, dark, dark eyes . . .

She smiled sleepily. Within seconds she had drifted off to sleep.

Hours later the warm June sun streamed in through the window, waking her. She threw the garden-patch quilt back to let her body soak in the sunshine. The rain had given way to the quiet brightness of a late spring morning. Sarah felt confident, recharged, no longer blind or vulnerable. She grabbed her glasses and sprang out of the pine-framed bed and pushed aside the stenciled tab curtains. She wanted to see where she was, where that long-ago Hamilton Blackstone had chosen to build his house.

High, white clouds billowed in a blue sky, and the lawns and meadows and forest and mountains that stretched endlessly before her seemed so lush and green and inviting. The bleak gray landscape of Manhattan was distant and unreal by comparison.

Sarah smiled and, peering closer at the Craigs' yard, could easily imagine why that first Hamilton Blackstone had chosen to build in this spot almost two hundred years ago. The hundreds of irises in dozens of colors and shapes that covered a flower garden off to her right wouldn't have been there, but perhaps those early Blackstones had had a neat, circular herb garden like the Craigs'.

The memory of her catnip-laden eggs thrust Sarah back into the twentieth century. She shook her head adamantly. No, she would not rehash every word of her mixed-up, infuriating conversation with her host. When Brad Craig encountered his unexpected guest this morning, he would immediately realize his mistake. He would see her refreshed, dry, fully dressed, utterly self-confident.

A movement out the window off to her left caught her attention. Turning, she saw a clothesline and a tall man bent over, rummaging in a wicker basket. Brad Craig! She couldn't suppress a smile as she watched him pluck a piece of laundry from the basket, shake it, and add it to the wash already hanging on the line.

All at once she recognized the big red heart of an I LOVE NEW YORK T-shirt. She had brought one along. . . .

No, it couldn't be!

Her eyes widened as she scanned the rest of the laundry blowing in the wind, the clothes she had worn yesterday, the blue drawstring pants that she had crumpled up into her pack, her rugby shirt, her underwear.

"Oh, *no!*"

Sarah looked behind her and with a sinking feeling remembered that she had stalked upstairs with only Bradley Craig's monstrous terry-cloth bathrobe to wear. All her clothes had remained downstairs, no doubt wet and ripe for mildew. And Brad had decided to be helpful and had run them through the wash and was now hanging them on the line.

So much for having him encounter a fully dressed and utterly self-confident Sarah Blackstone, she thought grimly. Damn! She glanced back down at the line. He was almost finished. She watched him give each of three pairs of cotton lace-trimmed underpants a single clothespin. She knew he had three more to go. Her three size 34B bras were already flapping in the breeze.

"Steady, Blackstone, steady," she mumbled. "No need being embarrassed." After all, she thought, other people handled her clothes all the time. "But not big brutes who think they're quarterbacks!"

She smiled sardonically to herself. Of course, this proved Brad Craig was no football jock. Would the quarterback for the New York Novas get up early one June morning to wash and hang an uninvited guest's laundry?

But that name . . .

Again its familiarity tugged at her memory. If not a quarterback, what? Who?

She quickly grabbed the robe, pulled it on, tied it *very* tightly, and headed downstairs. There was no point in delaying the inevitable. She would have to confront him in that damn bathrobe again sooner or later. She wondered if she should pretend she hadn't seen him matter-of-factly clipping a clothespin to her underpants. She groaned as she flounced into the bright, sunlit kitchen.

Brad walked in the back door with the empty wicker basket, which Sarah didn't want to mention, and dropped it in a corner. He stopped suddenly when he saw her standing in the middle of the kitchen swathed in his bathrobe. He didn't speak. He didn't have to. His eyes sought hers and found them behind her big square glasses. Then his gaze moved downward, taking in all it could: the softness of her slender neck and the long triangle of exposed collar and breastbone, where the floppy robe wouldn't stay put; the curve of her waist where the tie was securely knotted; the fabric that flowed from her waist and hid her long legs from his view; even her toes peeking out from under the dragging hem.

He made no attempt—not even the slightest—to be circumspect about his appraisal. Why bother? He thought she had come to seduce him—or to do all she could to have him seduce her—so why would he have a single qualm about looking at her however he damn well pleased? What surprised Sarah was that he damn well pleased to look at her in that manner. His gaze traveled back the way it had come, just as slowly and sensually, and rested again on her face, his look frankly sexy, approving of what he saw.

Sarah was neither embarrassed nor indignant—

another surprise to her—but instead captivated by the dusky desire in his eyes and the little twitch of amusement in his mouth. An unexpected but deliciously disconcerting ache arose within her—and all from a look, a grin. What would happen, she wondered, if he decided he had no qualms about touching her either?

"Morning," he said in a voice thick with sensuality, the twitch breaking into a broad smile as if he knew what she was wondering, expected it, and was delighted at how right he was.

"Uh—good morning," she said brightly and smiled, tearing her eyes from his. She was feeling a little light-headed. Hunger, she told herself firmly; it must be hunger. "I thought you might have slept late."

"Eight thirty," he said. "I like getting up and around when I'm in the country."

She glanced at the clock and saw it was after ten. "So do I usually, but this morning . . . I mean—"

"No, no. I don't blame you for sleeping late after you trek up here yesterday." His teasing was subtle, but unmistakable. He leaned his narrow hips against the counter and nodded at her. "If you're wondering where your clothes are—"

"Yes, I saw you," she said, a little too sharply. She smiled and raked her fingers through her hair. "From the bedroom window. You didn't—" She licked her lips. She was Sarah Blackstone, dammit! She met his dark, laughing eyes. "I am sure I could have managed, Mr. Craig."

His smile twisted sensually, knowingly. "No problem."

He paused, but Sarah had nothing to say.

"I expect it would have been hard hanging clothes in that." He gestured at the mammoth robe. "And I can't see using a dryer on a day like today myself. I like hanging clothes. It's relaxing. Hungry?"

She nodded and found herself becoming a bit

more comfortable. He definitely was *not* a football player. "Starved. I can fix myself something—"

"There's pancake batter in the fridge, but I don't know, Sarah." He folded his arms across his massive chest and shook his head thoughtfully as he scanned the slender figure swamped in his rust-colored robe. "Maybe I'd better fix you breakfast this one time. I wouldn't want you to catch yourself on fire or lose your robe or anything." He laughed and winked. "Wouldn't want to tempt me now, would you, Sarah?"

His mocking tone and frankly sensual gaze told her in no uncertain terms that a night's rest and reflection hadn't led Brad Craig to believe her story any more than he had when she told it. She narrowed her eyes and gave him one of her infamous penetrating looks, but his sexy grin didn't waver. His dark hair was tousled, the matching eyes gleaming with mischief, and his powerful body was clad in white duck pants and a loose-fitting sailor shirt. She could *almost* imagine herself thinking up ways to meet a man so good-looking and charming and at the same time, so very earthy and sensual.

But she *hadn't*!

"Something wrong, Sar?"

Her eyes leveled on him again. "Mr. Craig," she said, using the cool voice her mother and aunt had taught her so well, "I thought I made it clear last night that I do not appreciate your outrageous insinuations. I do admit my entrance may have been slightly offbeat—"

A thick eyebrow went up at the same time both corners of that firm mouth went down. "Slightly?"

She answered him by taking an extra breath before she resumed talking, another trick she had garnered from the Blackstone women. "It was, however, quite genuine. I bicycled up here from New York to stay with your parents."

This time the corners of his mouth went up,

and Sarah could see his tongue dragging along the inside of his lower lip. "You want to run through all your titles again?"

She stiffened. He didn't even believe *that* much? "My 'titles' have nothing to do with how and why I arrived here in the Catskills, Mr. Craig." She meant to sound haughty, but instead sounded flustered. Her bathrobe was slipping at the neckline. "I am who I said I am."

"Right, Sar."

Right, Sar. Damn, he wasn't going to believe her. He was *determined* not to believe her. She lifted the excess yards of terry cloth and flounced over to the bench. Without a word—only the deepest of chuckles—Brad pulled his long body from the counter and strode over to her. He grabbed her robe at the back of the neck and gave a little tug, and his touch—the brush of his knuckles along her hairline—was stimulating enough to whirl Sarah around. His eyes twinkled merrily when she almost tripped headlong into him. "Your collar was turned under."

"Oh." She gave a little laugh but knew she hadn't concealed her reaction to his touch very well.

Slowly, with deliberate casualness, his fingers—he used both hands now, one on each shoulder—grasped the collar and smoothed it down, first at her neck, then her collarbone.

"Mr. Craig—"

"Brad," he said, neither commanding nor pleading, merely stating his preference.

"Brad, I—"

She interrupted herself. Her whirl had opened the robe, exposing a hint of soft white breasts and the sensitive skin between them. Realizing this had pushed whatever she had meant to say from her thoughts. Brad turned the collar down over her breasts, his fingers firm and erotic even through the terry cloth, touching her nipples as if it were perfectly coincidental, though he knew they were naked beneath the baggy robe, yearning for his caress. He brought the right and left collars together, exactly in the middle of her breasts, and closed off his view with a noble bow.

"I'm not an animal, Sarah Blackstone," he said, his eyes suddenly no longer twinkling, "but I am a man, and few men I know could resist what you're offering."

Outraged and suddenly alert, Sarah drew back and clutched the robe together when his hands fell away. "I'm not offering you anything!"

He looked at her steadily, not moving an inch. "Aren't you? You didn't exactly pull back in indignation just now, Sar."

Sarah whirled back around and sat on the corner of the bench. No, she hadn't pulled back in indignation. But dammit, she was a woman and how was she supposed to resist what *he* was offering?

She watched surreptitiously from the corner of the bench as he dug a metal bowl out of the refrigerator, kicked the door shut with one heel, and crossed to the counter. His back to her, he picked through the utensils in a crock and settled on a long-handled wooden spoon. Inadvertently her eyes dropped to his narrow hips, his tight buttocks, the bulge of his thighs. . . .

No! Sarah coughed and shook her head. No, she would not allow herself to be drawn physically to this man. That was what he wanted and expected. Then he could throw it up in her face and say, "See, you did engineer your entrance just to meet me!"

She watched as he stirred the batter. "You may not believe me, Mr. Craig," she began, sounding cool now, "but you might be surprised to know that I don't believe you either."

"No?"

He dusted his hands off on his pants. Sarah could hear the hard, callused hands meeting the muscles of his thighs. What if she were wrong? Who *but* an athlete would have such a body?

"No," she averred. "A quarterback wouldn't have gotten up early and washed and hung clothes, his own *or* someone else's, and certainly not those of a woman whom he is convinced is trying"—she would *not* blush or hesitate!—"to seduce him."

Brad seemed amused. "And what would he have done?"

"He would have used the damn dryer!"

"I see." He opened up the griddle on the counter and plugged it in. "So you don't believe I'm Brad Craig?"

Sarah smiled smugly. "I don't believe you're the Novas' quarterback."

He laughed. "You're a riot, Sar."

"Don't call me that!" She reacted more vehemently than she had meant to, but his irreverent "Sar" curled up her spine like smoke. She calmed herself, but her voice was still strained when she continued. "Of course, what we believe or don't believe about each other is irrelevant. I'm only interested in conducting my research on the Blackstone cemetery. I would at least like to see it before I leave. Will you permit me?"

As he mindlessly continued to stir the batter Brad looked around, his brow furrowed slightly, and silently studied Sarah. She had reined in her temper quickly, he mused, as if she were used to bottling up her feelings to achieve a goal. As a professional, he had done the same himself, many times. He was surprised and more than a little intrigued by the woman who seemed to be so patient while waiting for his answer. He was dying to find out who she really was.

At last he shrugged. "I suppose it wouldn't be very noble of me to send a woman with strained hamstrings back out on her bicycle."

This time Sarah couldn't read his tone. She sensed he was backing off slightly, putting some distance between himself and her story, or at least his reaction to it. He wasn't mocking her, but he wasn't entirely serious either. Suspicious? Worried? Annoyed? She couldn't tell.

"Mr. Craig," she said softly, "*are* you a football player?"

His eyes, still fixed on hers, opened in surprise just as he burst into deep, free laughter.

Sarah spun around toward the table, but the robe twisted between her legs before she could get them completely over the bench. Why was he laughing? A moment ago she had sensed a shield—perhaps one as strong as her own—going up, but now he was laughing with such zest and delight that Sarah couldn't help but smile. She struggled to free herself from the tangles of the robe. Was he amused because she hadn't recognized him as the Novas' quarterback—or because she had swallowed enough of his story even to ask?

She tore at the robe and accidentally exposed one long, slender leg to Brad's view. Her face instantly felt hot. She didn't look up, but the sudden halt of his laughter told her he had noticed. The leg was bare to the thigh. She quickly covered it and, holding the robe firmly in place, lifted the leg and gracefully planted it under the table. She folded her hands primly on the tabletop and didn't say a word. During her entire, exhausting trip yesterday she had never considered that seeing the tombstones of her ancestors wasn't worth all the trouble. Now she did.

"Oh, Sarah, Sarah," Brad said in a voice deep with mocking awe, "you're a clever one, aren't you?"

The shield was back up again. Somehow another outburst seemed inappropriate. She clamped her mouth shut and judiciously said nothing.

He laughed but without the zest of a moment ago. "Okay, Sar, you can stay."

She turned halfway around on the bench, careful to keep both legs tucked under the table, and observed him as he ran his fingertips under the faucet. He flicked drops of water onto the griddle and watched them sizzle and evaporate. She noticed the tensed muscles and dark curly hairs of his long forearms. Her fingertips tingled, telling her how much they longed to touch those arms and feel their strength. Brad glanced at her and half grinned knowingly, as if he guessed what she was thinking and wasn't surprised.

The conceited ox, she thought.

But no, it was more complicated than that. *He* was more complicated. She sensed caution, if not fear; an unwilling and unnatural distrust not simply of her, but of any woman who had appeared so mysteriously on his doorstep at midnight.

Why wouldn't he believe her story? Why that caution? Who was he that he needed to distrust her? She looked again at the forearms and the tall, muscular body. She tried to be objective and ignored the tightness in her throat. He looked to be around six feet three and ten or fifteen pounds over two hundred. Big. But big enough, strong enough, agile enough to be the quarterback for the Novas?

Undoubtedly.

Certainly that *could* explain his caution. How many women had stalked the Novas' quarterback? So what initially seemed so egotistical to her could simply be a reaction, a cynicism born out of his past. Perhaps he wanted to believe her, Sarah mused, but his experience with "mysterious" appearances forced him to be suspicious.

He began humming as he ladled dollops of batter onto the hot griddle. No. A quarterback *wouldn't* wash and hang out a strange woman's clothes! She shook off her thoughts and retied the robe. What was it he had said? She could stay. Of course.

"Thank you," she said at last. "I'll try not to get in your way."

His answering, skeptical grin pierced the terry-cloth and went straight to her. He was *gorgeous!* But no. She had come to the Catskills to relax and do research on the Blackstone cemetery. And Brad Craig—whoever he was—was obviously not going to believe her story. Whether it was conceit or cynicism or simple caution that made him disbelieving didn't matter. She had *not* ridden her bicycle all the way into the heart of the Catskills for a "toss in the hay" with a hulking athlete.

Brad brought her a plate of steaming pancakes, a pitcher of syrup he declared he had made himself that March, butter, and coffee. He filled his mug, and with a satisfied sigh dropped into the chair at the end of the table near Sarah. He smiled at her as she spread butter over the pancakes. "With all these people making you breakfast, you're going to get spoiled," he said, gesturing at her with his mug. "Didn't your friends make you waffles yesterday morning?"

The *supposedly* was implicit in his question, but Sarah pretended not to notice. The pancakes were wonderful, and he had been kind enough to make them for her . . . and to hang her wash. She grinned back at him and nodded.

"Actually I'm already spoiled. I don't have pancakes and homemade maple syrup every morning, but I do have my own cook." She popped a forkful of the light pancakes in her mouth. "Comes with being a Blackstone."

"Does it now?"

Brad grinned so broadly that the corners of his eyes crinkled and most of his even white teeth showed. Sarah had to struggle to keep from staring. It wasn't a perfect face—she noticed a tough scar above his left eyebrow—but it radiated all the charm and earthiness and sensuality that seemed more a part of him, more natural, than the cynicism and conceit. She quickly swallowed her pancakes, not having chewed them properly.

"Well, I'll say this for you, Sar: You are tenacious," he said, laughing freely again. "You're like a little bulldog chewing an old shoe to pieces. You just won't let go. I suppose the president of this Blackstone Industries and chairman of this Blackstone Foundation of yours would have a cook, but tell me, would she show up at someone's house at midnight, soaked to the bone and half blind?"

Sarah sighed and concentrated on her pancakes. A bulldog, she repeated to herself. The man had just compared her to a bulldog. *That* had never happened in her near thirty years.

"I explained why I was wet," she said, dipping a forkful of pancakes in a tiny pool of syrup. "My eyesight is hereditary. I can't help it."

She looked up, expecting to see caution and cynicism, to confront that shield or his teasing grin. Instead, she saw that his gaze was on her, taking in not only her face now, but her smooth hands, the curve of her lean figure draped in the robe, the depths of her soul.

He leaned over the table toward her and with one finger touched each of the well-manicured but short, unpolished nails of her left hand, which had been lying next to her plate. Then the finger ran up her middle finger, along the knuckles, and then up the fine bone all the way to the middle of her wrist. She watched, mesmerized; awed at how gentle the touch of such a big man could be . . . and how fantastically erotic one finger with its light, sensuous stroking could be. Her hand sent out frantic messages of excitement to the rest of her body, and she had to will herself to keep still and not grab his hand and press it to her.

"I've never met a chairman of the board as young and beautiful as you are, Sarah Blackstone," he said quietly, almost ominously, his tone at odds with his almost delicate caress.

Her eyes bored into his. She wouldn't flinch. "That's your misfortune, Mr. Craig," she said coolly.

"I assure you, women who moon over football players aren't the only ones who are attractive."

The probing look vanished, and he grinned and pulled his hand back. "Sar, if even half the women who've chased after me the past fifteen or twenty years had been nearly as good-looking and smart-assed as you are, I'd probably have been snared by one of them by now." He rose suddenly, mug in hand, and reached a long arm toward her. A callused thumb brushed one of her high cheek-bones and sounded countless tiny alarms all through her body. "I might as well warn you, Sar. I'm not an easy man to snare."

His hand dropped back down to his side, and slowly the alarms quieted. She stared at him in shock. He was *serious*!

"Mr. Craig, you're being unfair. You're jumping to conclusions."

He shrugged. "Maybe."

"You know, you're casting *all* women into the role of conniving little harlots—"

"Not *all* women," he said mildly. "I'm not a chauvinist. Just women who do bizarre things to meet me and tell lies to impress me. And men. I told you last night both men and women have done strange things just to meet me." He started toward the hall.

"Dammit, I *am* Sarah Blackstone!" she yelled. "I wouldn't need to go to all this trouble just to meet you!"

"That's it, Sar," he called back. "Don't give up!"

"I'll prove it to you! Come with me to the cemetery and—"

Just his head poked back into the kitchen. "Sarah, you *know* there isn't a single Blackstone buried up here."

"I know no such thing!"

Brad grinned, patted the woodwork, and was gone. "If you don't believe me," she shouted after him, "why are you letting me stay?"

Because you're so damned intriguing . . . so determined and yet so vulnerable, Brad said to himself. *And dammit, because I want you! I've known you less than twenty-four hours, Sarah Blackstone, and I don't know who the devil you really are and what you want with me, but I do know how much I want to touch and hold you. . . .*

He hesitated in the hall, but decided against answering her aloud. He had been burned badly before, and if Sarah Blackstone was another conniving woman, he had to contend with—

But she *wasn't!* Brad told himself. He knew it. Why else had he just permitted her to stay? He growled and stomped off down the hall.

When Brad didn't answer, Sarah huffed and hoped her brother had been right. Because if there weren't any Blackstones buried on the grounds— indeed, if her brother had given her the wrong information, and this wasn't even the old Blackstone estate—then she would have to do some fast backtracking with Herr Craig.

She hoped big brother Hamilton hadn't decided to have a bit of fun with his little sister. . . .

Three

Two hours later Sarah was sitting in the tall thick grass, still damp from yesterday's rain, with her pad and clipboard in her lap and her pen sideways between her lips. Hamilton hadn't tricked her or been mistaken. She ran her fingertips along the warn granite of Sarah Elizabeth Blackstone's headstone. She had died in childbirth at age thirty-four. The baby was buried beside her.

Tears welled in the latter-day Sarah's eyes. Had tragedy been the Blackstone fate even two hundred years ago? Were they all destined to die early deaths? Or only the good ones, the strong ones, the ones who could leave behind people who loved and needed them?

Sarah felt the tears hot on her cheeks, the sun's heat on her neck, the cool dampness of the grass seeping into the seat of her cotton drawstring pants. She hadn't expected to be so moved by the remains of these long-dead ancestors. This was to have been an intellectual endeavor—an excuse, even, for going on this unusual vacation. Her lark. For too long her life had been dominated by struggle and responsibility—all work and no play. She wanted to achieve a balance, put her struggles and responsibilities into perspective. She had to! But the lives of these dead forefathers and mothers touched hers. They had been real people. Their blood ran in her veins. She was their future.

Maybe this was all to the good, she thought. By touching the past, perhaps she could right her present. She brushed away her tears, pulled the pen from her lips, and jotted down the information on the headstone, and then the one beside it. There were approximately twenty-five headstones in all, although not all were Blackstones.

At last, hot and hungry and stiff but oddly at peace, she crawled onto the stone wall that surrounded the cemetery. She breathed deeply the country air and unwrapped her peanut butter and jelly sandwich. All things considered, her morning had gone well. She had avoided Brad Craig, or he had avoided her, and had managed to remove her laundry from the line herself, dress in peace, and make herself a sandwich without having to contend with his doubting, teasing grin or even her frustration at having his name seem so familiar and yet unidentifiable. She had decided to let the matter of his identity rest.

She groaned low when she started on the second half of her sandwich and saw his tall figure ambling across the lawn. "What now?" she wondered aloud.

And yet she felt an ache, a stirring in the pit of her stomach as she watched a breeze catch the tendrils of his dark, dark hair. She tried to resist it for no more reason than pride. She didn't want him to think she might fall victim to his undeniable sensual charms, and yet he must know, for she had told him in so many not exactly subtle ways.

He waved at her, and even twenty yards away, in the bright June sun, she could see—feel—his sexy, mischievous grin. She didn't wave back. She was busy reminding herself that, according to *his* version of last night, she already did want to go to bed with him. She would have to remember that.

"So," he said as he approached the stone wall, "you really are going through with this."

She smiled. "It's the bulldog in me."

He looked down at her and laughed with delight. Then he scanned the hodgepodge of worn headstones within the stone wall. So she hadn't lied about that, he thought.

"I guess you've done your research," he said amiably.

Sarah looked smug. He lifted a sneakered foot onto the rock next to hers and shifted his weight onto his bent leg. The long, muscled leg was just inches from her shoulder. He didn't have to stand so close—Sarah knew it and suspected he did as well—but what better way to tempt her? She wasn't immune. She couldn't deny that she yearned to touch the thickness of his thighs and measure their hardness with her fingertips. She had not lied about who she was and her reasons for being in the Catskills, but she was not made of stone. She was a woman and he—

Her gaze flickered to the fabric drawn tight over the muscles of his legs. Her throat suddenly seemed so constricted, her breathing so shallow. Yes, she was a woman, and he—oh, God, he was a man.

He noticed her reaction, but pretended not to. "This place is crawling with dead Blackstones, isn't it? I might have recognized the Blackstone name, Sarah, but this is only my second or third time up here and I don't usually go around checking to see who's buried on the property."

"That's understandable." If she didn't look at those legs, or those laughing eyes, or that grin—if she didn't look at *him*, she would be all right. But why, she wondered, did she want to be all right? Oh, to lose herself in those eyes! If only he would believe her. . . . "Then you believe my story?"

She was looking at the half of the sandwich in her lap, but knew he was smiling teasingly, doubtingly. "Not entirely," he said. "Let's just say you've presented me with an even more compelling mystery."

"I am not presenting you with *any* mystery! Look, Brad—"

"You're slipping, Sar. What happened to 'Mr. Craig'?"

She raised her eyes to his face fully intending to give him one of her famous haughty looks, but the sight of his gleaming eyes and the sun dancing on his dark hair caught her off guard. Her pale green eyes softened and her mouth drew in air to ease an overwhelming feeling of breathlessness. She turned away too quickly.

Brad tucked two fingers beneath her chin and turned her face back to him, tilting it upward. If only she had remembered to call him Mr. Craig! But Brad felt so right. His fingers no longer held her face toward his, but she didn't turn away, and they touched her chin then pressed lightly on her lips, as if those two callused fingertips were his lips meeting hers.

"Your nose is getting sunburned," he said languidly. "You should wear a hat."

He tapped her nose with his index finger and pushed up her glasses. "If I wore a hat," she said, a little breathlessly, "my hair would get all flat and limp."

He touched the hair at her forehead that was slightly damp from her morning of work. "Then we'll have to dig you out some sunscreen," he said, his lazy, lilting tone belying the matter-of-factness of his words. "I'm sure my mother has some around somewhere—"

As Sarah prepared to answer, his mouth descended quickly, almost from nowhere, and brushed hers lightly, but not at all tentatively. A low growl rumbled in his throat, and his lips sought hers again, finding them. His fingers slid through her hair and cupped the roundness of her shoulder, then darted lower and just grazed her breast. The nipple hardened beneath his touch, uncontradictable evidence of her deepest reaction to him.

His mouth drew away from hers, but stayed so close, she could feel his breath when he spoke. "Well, Sar," he said, "was that worth a hundred-mile trek up here on a bicycle—or do you want more?"

He was teasing her, but the duskiness of his eyes warned Sarah he had been as aroused as she. It was a heady thought, but pleasing. This was her lark, she reminded herself, and Brad Craig had two kind, generous parents. He was no beast. Hadn't he said so himself? She smiled. "You're a funny man, Mr. Bradley Craig," she said and began eating her sandwich again.

"Is that so?" he asked sardonically, and she knew he was grinning. Out of the corner of her eye she saw that the sneakered foot had been removed from the stone wall. He cast a shadow deeper than that of the elm tree as he turned and sat down beside her. Although her rock was higher, he still had at least an inch on her. "You're not answering any of my questions, Sarah," he said, obviously pleased that she was obviously flustered. "Want me to tell you about the mystery you've presented?"

She balled up the little plastic bag and finished off the sandwich. "Not particularly."

"Tut-tut."

He casually stretched out his long legs. For some reason unfathomable to her, Sarah's gaze fastened on the exposed part of his ankles, between the hem of his pants and the top of his sneakers, glimpsing dark hair and tanned skin. Even his damn ankles radiated the power of an athlete! She squeezed the plastic bag tightly in her fist as she wondered what it would be like to run her toes along those ankles. . . .

"So here's my problem," he said. "I'm wondering what your *real* name is."

Sarah tore her gaze from his ankles, cleared her throat, and began smoothing the crumpled plastic on one knee. Her fingers were clammy. But she reminded herself that she had had years of practice at being cool and collected in the most trying of situations. She looked at Brad and said with regal aloofness, "I told you. My name is Sarah Blackstone, and I am president and chief executive officer of Blackstone Industries and chairman of the board of the Blackstone Foundation. If you would like to call my office and assure yourself of my credentials, I will be happy to give you the number."

She wouldn't be *happy* to do it, Sarah thought— she could just imagine the gossip such a call would generate—but she hoped the offer would be enough to knock him off his high horse.

"Sure," he replied, "and I'll just bet it'll be the number of some friend of yours—"

Sarah leaped off the rock and whirled about at him. "Look up the number then! Our headquarters are on East Fiftieth Street."

He grinned, unruffled. "But of course."

"I *am* Sarah Blackstone! I'll show you my driver's license."

That got him. He crossed one arm, placed the elbow of his other arm in its palm, and pensively rubbed his chin with the thumb of his outstretched hand. His index finger popped up as a light came into his eyes. He chuckled. "Oh, you *are* good, Sarah," he said, shaking his head in wonder. He stretched his arms out straight and placed a hand on each knee. "Okay, so you're Sarah Blackstone. You knew about the cemetery, heard I'd bought this place for my parents when they retired, and decided to take advantage of your ancestry and thought up this escapade to meet me. Pretty clever."

Sarah groaned. "I'll try *once* more." She paced back and forth two feet in front of him with her arms crossed over her breasts. "I have long been interested in tracing the Blackstone family tree, but with all my responsibilities—which have only gotten worse in the last year—I have had little time to indulge my interest."

"Why so many responsibilities?"

She stopped pacing. "Because of the Blackstone tragedy," she said baldly. "I *am* young, Mr. Craig, to be in my position within the company and the foundation, but for a reason. Five years ago my father and uncle were killed in a sailing accident. That left only me and my brother capable and willing to take over, so we did."

There was more to the story than that, but Sarah didn't bother to give all the details. If Brad wanted to know more, he could look up the story in any library that had back issues of weekly magazines and New York newspapers. She had given him the gist of that horrible day and its aftermath, and how much it had changed her life.

He motioned for her to go on.

"Several weeks ago I learned about this house and cemetery." She paused to curse her brother silently for ever telling her. "I contacted the current owners—your parents—and they consented to let me stay here for a few days and do some research. I told them who I was, and *they* believed me."

She stopped and glanced at Brad. His eyes were laughing and the curve of those lips was sardonic and amused. "Mum and Dad are like that. Go on."

She braced herself and continued. "Not being a football fan, I did *not* know that their son is—or thinks he is—a quarterback. Nor did I know they had a daughter, never mind that she was pregnant and due anytime." Her voice rose steadily in spite of her resolve to stay calm. "And I most especially, certainly, absolutely did *not* know that I would end up trying to explain all this to a big, leering, impossible, *grinning* jock who won't believe a word I say!"

Brad casually folded his muscular arms on his chest, his dark, dark eyes still laughing, and ran his tongue from one inside corner of his mouth to the other. "Now, Sar," he said mildly, "I haven't once leered at you."

Oh, God, Sarah thought. A blush crept up her throat and into her cheeks. She felt hot, flushed, livid, drained. Had she said *leering*? *Damn!* She spun around in the grass and started vaguely toward the house, somewhere—anywhere—away from Brad Craig.

"If you're so short on time and such a busy lady, why did you bicycle all the way up here?" he asked, his tone steady and confident, just this side of cocky. "How come you didn't just hire some penniless academic research assistant to come copy the info off the headstones?"

She didn't turn around. "This is my vacation!"

"Well, it's one hell of a way to spend a vacation, Sarah. I would think a corporate president, especially one as pretty and elegant as you, would trot herself to Paris or Rome or some place like that for a vacation."

She refused to explain. There was no point. Her own mother hadn't believed her explanation. So why would a man who didn't even really accept her as being Sarah Blackstone believe it? She kept walking.

Brad followed. He was beside her in an instant, matching every two of her angry, clipped steps with one of his long, easy strides.

"I was wrong," he said, and at Sarah's quizzical, still-angry look, he chuckled. "You're not so elegant. No corporate types I know—not to mention elegant ladies—would stalk off leaving a leering jock like me a view of her wet behind." He patted that wet behind. "Not elegant, Sar."

"Will you *stop*?"

More in exasperation than anger she whirled halfway around and grabbed his wrist. Her fingers curled as far around its iron muscles and bone as they could.

"Not bad, Sar," he said, glancing down at the wrist held tightly in her fingers. "You're pretty quick."

"Quick, but ultimately ineffective," she muttered, and still holding on, sighed tiredly. "Bradley—"

"Just Brad, and I know. Hands off, right? You don't want me to touch you anymore."

Thinking he had taken her seriously this time, she nodded solemnly. If she persisted, sooner or later he would have to accept her story. But when she looked up at him, his eyes were gleaming and he was having difficulty smothering yet another grin. *He didn't believe her!*

She inhaled sharply. "I *don't* want you to touch me!"

"Sure, Sar."

He looked meaningfully at his wrist, where her fingers were lingering much longer than was necessary. She snatched them away, as if his wrist had suddenly turned to fire. He smiled, pleased with himself.

She opened her mouth to explain once more, but stopped herself when she saw something pass through those brown eyes that hadn't been there a moment before. Half closed, they were studying her. She, in turn, was studying him. Neither turned away from the other's probing gaze. The bright sun had brought out the unexpected golden highlights of his dark hair, but also laid bare the lines of his strong face, the skin toughened by years of exposure to the weather. The inch-long scar above his left eye seemed to glare at her and give that brow a frowning cast.

She could believe he was a quarterback. At that moment she could believe almost anything he cared to tell her. She couldn't tear her gaze from his face. It had the kind of ruggedness and honesty—and depth—that could hold her interest for hours, years.

What could he see in her face, in her eyes? The strange loneliness that had overcome her, the longing? Could he see her lie? She did want him to touch her. It was that simple, that undeniable. She wanted to touch him, to hold him, to let his earthiness and sensuality overpower the shield she held up. If only for a little while she wanted to forget. She wanted to play. And why not? Sarah asked herself. Wasn't that why she had come to the Catskills to begin with? To find that elusive balance between work and play, between freedom and responsibility?

"Sarah."

His voice was quiet, just above a whisper. She

smiled almost sadly. She supposed she should say something curt and pointed, cool and regal. Nothing came. Brad touched her cheek, then snuggled his outstretched fingers into the curve of her neck. She didn't pull away.

"Oh, Sarah."

With the briefest flicker in his eyes, as if he had told himself he ought to know better, he lowered his mouth, pausing just before his lips touched hers. She could have pulled away, but she didn't. She said nothing. She didn't even breathe. His hand still nestled in her neck, he covered her mouth with his.

His lips were warm, dry from the sun and the wind, gentle. Sarah closed her eyes and absorbed everything about the kiss—the feel, the promise, the longing.

His hands shot around her waist and pulled her to him, his thumbs digging into her sides. Her body molded against his, began to loosen, relax, her shield shattering as she knew only the taste of his lips and the hardness of his big body against hers. His mouth claimed hers more fully. *Brad, Brad, where have you been all these months, all these years?* Her lips parted, welcoming the heat and wetness of his tongue.

With the deepening of their kiss his hands crept upward until they were at her ribs, his long thumbs just beneath her breasts. With a slow, expert motion they gently circled and caressed each swelling nipple until she moaned into his mouth and moved erotically against him, her body telling him all he needed to know. She wanted him to touch her everywhere.

Brad broke the kiss slowly, pulling away and straightening. "I think there might be more to you than I thought, Sarah Blackstone," Brad said quietly. His eyes weren't laughing now, his mouth wasn't grinning. He was breathing hard, as hungry for more of her as she was of him. "Either you're *very* good at playing a man for a fool, or you're sincere." He lifted a hand toward her, but before he touched her, he quickly shoved both hands in his pockets. "I've been burned so damn many times—" He bit off his words and looked up at the sky. "I may be crazy, Sarah, but I'd like to get to know you better."

Sarah took a deep breath, trying to recover from all that he had awakened within her. "The me you *think* I am, or the me I really am?" she asked pointedly. He shot a look down at her. Sarah smiled. It was her turn to tease him. "I'm not at all sure you've earned the right to get to know me, Bradley Craig."

His brows arched in surprise, even as his laugh erupted. Without warning he pressed his index finger to one side of her cheek, then the other. "Dimples!" he exclaimed, delighted. "Now tell me what stuffy old corporate president and chairman of the board *you* know who has dimples!"

"I can't help it if I have dimples! I—I—" She gritted her teeth and groaned. "You're impossible!"

He laughed again. "Have dinner with me tonight, Sarah. You can drag out all your evidence to prove who you are."

"You have *got* to be kidding! After what just happened—what's *been* happening?" She shook her head. It was far too late to pretend to have been insulted by his kiss, but she didn't have to tell him how it had weakened her knees, weakened them still. "Uh-uh, no way. I'm going to ride into town and find a restaurant and—"

"And there isn't a restaurant within ten miles of here that's more than a breakfast and lunch place," he interrupted. "Are you sure your hamstrings are up to a twenty-mile ride? I'd offer you my car, but I'd rather have you stay for dinner. You're fun, Sar." The grin was back, taunting, unabashedly sensual.

Sarah pursed her lips and called forth all the

determination and restraint of her Blackstone
breeding. The idea of dinner alone with this man
combined with the lingering warmth of his kiss
tempted her to say yes. *Are you crazy, Blackstone?*
"That's—I—" She needed a reason and fast. She
swallowed. She had it! "I don't want to be a burden,
Brad. I—"

"No problem." He rubbed his jaw. "Look, my
folks' cook is coming in to fix dinner anyway. He's
five six and weighs two hundred pounds and car-
ries a meat cleaver the size of an ax. So, sweetheart,
if I try anything you don't *want* me to try—"

"You conceited baboon!" But she was already
nodding in acceptance. "Okay, okay, I'll be there."

"Good." He patted her on the behind. "Back to
work, Madam Chairman."

She covered her wet seat where his hand had
touched her and opened her mouth to protest,
but already his powerful, agile figure was trotting
down the hill. His gait was light and easy. Victorious. Sarah frowned. But what victory did he
think he had won? She shook her head in wonder
and returned to the cemetery.

Four

That evening Sarah found Brad alternately humming and singing as he minced chives with a
giant knife at the kitchen counter. Pointedly clearing her throat but simultaneously holding back a
smile, she folded her arms across her breasts so

that her long, thin fingers were splayed on her upper arms. He looked around and gave a grin that went right through her, reminding her of his kiss, his charm, everything that made her want to smile back and be glad she wasn't pedaling toward a restaurant.

"You're not five six," she stated.

He shrugged. "And I'm a few pounds over two hundred, but I'm one hell of a cook."

Sarah recalled the catnip-laden eggs, which were awful, and then the pancakes, which were wonderful. Her doubt found its way to her face. One corner of her mouth twisted upward and her brow furrowed.

"Well, I have my specialties," Brad admitted. "Lime tarragon chicken and stir-fried anything." He waved the knife absently. "I've been known to stir-fry old shoelaces."

Sarah couldn't catch her smile before it started across her face. "Yummy."

He resumed mincing the chives. "Don't fret, you're getting the lime tarragon chicken."

"Fresh tarragon?"

"Yeah. Apparently it came back this year with a vengeance. The garden's crawling with the stuff. Can't you smell it?"

She sniffed the air, which indeed held the rich, pungent scent of tarragon. "I should never doubt you, should I?" She walked over to the sink and stood along the counter, about two feet away from Brad and his knife. "Can I help? If I'd known this cook of yours was a myth—"

"You wouldn't have come," he finished.

"A woman who bicycled an entire day in the pouring rain just to meet you would turn down an invitation to dinner?"

He looked over at her from the chopping block, the knife suspended in midair. "No, I suppose not," he said, but before Sarah could clap her hands in victory, he went on. "However, a woman who desperately wants me to believe she *didn't* bicycle an entire day in the pouring rain just to meet me might turn down an invitation to dinner just to make me wonder." He waved the knife at her. "And you'll notice you *are* here."

He eyed her with such frankness and appreciation that any incipient anger quickly disappeared. She had to straighten her knees to keep them from weakening and sagging. She placed a hand on the edge of the sink and steadied herself. She had bathed and dressed in a red-striped top and the lightweight white skirt she had packed "just in case." The sandals and absence of stockings added to the casualness of her appearance, but she had clearly taken time with her gleaming hair, combing it so that it had dried perfectly straight. And her face glowed with touches of blusher and lip gloss.

"So why didn't you call my bluff?" she asked. "I would have thought you'd find it amusing to see how I got out of finding a restaurant."

He hacked at the last inch of chives. "Two reasons. One, I'm on to you and you know it, so what better way to make me question myself than seeing you pedal off to a restaurant? Two"—he flicked the minced chives off the blade of his knife and narrowed his eyes at her for a moment—"I want to get to know you better, no matter who or what you are, so I gave you an out."

"How good of you."

But a sudden breathlessness, as though someone or something was pressing into her gut, had undermined Sarah's cool tone. She was losing control. Her throat grew tight with wondering what it would be like to lay her head on that broad chest and rub her hands up and down the warm cotton of his white-flecked navy sweater. She bit the inside corner of her mouth. He was toying with her, playing a warped game.

She licked her lips, but her eyes drifted downward to the crisp navy duck pants that could just accommodate the thickness of his thighs—the thighs of an athlete.

"I—you—" She sighed, annoyed with herself. "What can I do to help?"

He waved the knife at a milk carton full of scraps. "You can take that to the compost by the vegetable garden if you want."

"Gladly."

She hoped she didn't sound too relieved as she grabbed the carton and rushed out the door. Outside she inhaled the evening air, warm enough to be soothing, cool enough to be fresh. This had to stop, she thought. In a few short minutes Bradley Craig had managed to stretch every one of her nerves. Her entire body seemed to vibrate with an awareness of him. She could feel every beat of her pounding heart.

She marched toward the vegetable garden. Brad Craig wanted—expected—this reaction to him, and for that reason alone she should resist him. He knew so little about her and accepted none of it, and yet she couldn't ignore his insidious charm.

When she had finally given in to the ache in her lower back from crouching in front of headstones, Sarah had gone for a long walk through the fields and woods of the old Blackstone estate. While strolling through the lush green fields and listening to the birds chirp and the chipmunks and squirrels rustle in the brush, she had tried to rekindle some sense of indignation at Brad's teasing and doubt. Instead, she had imagined him in the blue and white of a Novas uniform and wondered if he, like her, wasn't lying about his identity. . . . But did it matter at all that she was the president of a corporation and that he was a quarterback?

After her walk she had gone back to the house and upstairs without seeing him. She had tried to read. She had tried to sleep. She had tried to tell herself that their dinner together was nothing that even resembled a date. This was to have been a time of healing and cleansing, not playing games with a man, even one as wonderful and tempting as Brad Craig.

And why not? She had asked herself that question over and over. Why not? She felt as though she'd been waiting all this time just to stumble into this place and into Brad's life. Their meeting could have been ordained by the gods, or at least the two dozen Blackstones buried on the property. Why fight it? Oh, she had told herself, she was being silly. It was the beautiful surroundings; delayed spring fever.

Nevertheless, she had taken a long, hot bath in the upstairs bathroom, scenting the water with a touch of Dorothy Craig's bath oil. She had thought of how easily she could forget all her awesome responsibilities with a man like Brad Craig. Her mother, her brother, her aunt, her young cousins . . . with Brad she could forget them and all they expected of her, and all she expected of herself.

But that wasn't the point of her solitary bike ride north! The point was for her to do all that *herself*. She couldn't lean on someone else or expect someone else to do it for her. She had to pick herself up by her own bootstraps and make herself whole again. No one could do it for her, certainly not a man she had known less than a day!

She had come downstairs not really expecting a two-hundred-pound cook, at least not one under six feet, and had been happy to see Brad. Comfortable. As though she had known him for years. He was one of those rare men with whom people automatically felt relaxed. She wondered how many life stories he had heard from people he hardly knew.

She turned the carton over and dumped it into the compost bin. "Sarah," she muttered aloud, "if the man *is* a football player, he's got *thousands* of women falling over him." She hit the bottom of the carton. "Good-looking athletes can afford to be charming. Think of all the women he's sized up over the years. All he's doing is figuring out what you want from him and giving it to you."

He had sized her up wrong. She checked the carton and scraped out the last bit of carrot peels with her fingers before starting back to the house.

Brad was setting one end of the table: one stoneware plate, fork, spoon, and knife for each of them. One place was at the end of the table, in front of a chair, and the other in front of the bench on the corner. With his long legs and the table trestle, Sarah thought, they would be avoiding each other's knees throughout dinner. Maybe not, though. She pulled in her lips, pushed them out, and dumped the empty carton in the trash.

"It's not very fancy," Brad said, "but it'll do. If you want candles, I'm sure you can scrounge up a pair in the dining room."

"No, no. This is lovely."

" 'Lovely'?" He lo0ked up and grinned. "You're a riot, Sar. Have a seat, I'll serve you. You must be used to that, right?"

He was teasing her again, laughing at her "story" without laughing. Sarah pulled out the bench and sat down. "As a matter of fact," she said regally, "I am."

He chuckled as he served dinner: his lime tarragon chicken, new potatoes sprinkled with parsley, carrots and chives, and fresh spinach salad. Dammit, she thought, why does he have to be so *nice*? A sexy, good-looking, conceited jerk she could resist, but a sexy, good-looking, charming man? She shivered.

Finally Brad sat down. His right knee touched Sarah's left knee. Very subtly, before the tingle in that knee could spread, she edged a few inches down the bench. When she glanced up, Brad's eyes were fastened on her. He wasn't chuckling now. She couldn't tell what had happened to the chuckle, or more particularly what had replaced it.

She gestured vaguely at the stoneware bowls and platter filled with the steaming food. "It makes a pretty meal, doesn't it?" she said with an uneasy smile. "I once prepared a dinner menu calling for broiled fish, boiled potatoes, and cauliflower with cheese sauce. It wasn't very picturesque, but fortunately Mrs. Friedrich noticed and—"

Her flow of chatter stopped at the sudden narrowing of Brad's eyes. The scar seemed to deepen his frown. It was a dark gaze, penetrating, and Sarah envisioned him intimidating an opposing team with those eyes. Weren't quarterbacks supposed to have quick, menacing eyes like that?

"Who are you, Sarah?"

The question startled her. She gave a stupid-sounding laugh. "I was just wondering the same thing about you." She clamped her mouth shut, annoyed with her nervousness. Her lips turned up in a light, sarcastic smile, but she knew her fingers were trembling. "I've already told you who I am—more than once."

"Damn persistent, aren't you?" He heaved a sigh, shook his head, and handed her the bowl of carrots. "If you're planning to make a fool out of me, Sarah Blackstone, you can damn well forget it, do you understand? I tend to remember things like that, and I *always* get my revenge."

The menacing look and the frown were gone, and he spoke almost casually, but Sarah could feel the underlying seriousness—the determination—of his words. She shrugged to show him she wasn't intimidated. "Mr. Craig, if I weren't utterly famished, I would dump this bowl of carrots in your lap." She spooned six of the tiny carrots onto her plate. "You may choose not to believe that what I say is true. I suppose that is your right. But you may *not* make unfounded accusations. I am not planning to make a fool out of you." She leveled the haughty gaze of the Blackstone women at him. "From my vantage point, Mr. Craig, you need no help at all from me."

He didn't laugh. He didn't leap up and snatch her by the ear and toss her out the front door. He didn't roar with anger. He simply and slowly cocked his head to one side and stared at her with a mixture of awe and incredulity and amusement. Sarah smiled and asked him to pass the potatoes.

With their coffee they had dessert—fresh strawberries—outside on the front porch. Brad sat on the wide railing, Sarah in a wicker chair. Their animosity had eased with her first taste of the lime tarragon chicken. She had insisted Brad give her a blow-by-blow description of how he had made it and vowed to get herself a pot of tarragon for the rooftop deck of her Manhattan town house. Brad had resisted asking her what a woman who had lost a contact lens in a mud puddle would do with a Manhattan town house, but told her how to make lime tarragon chicken. She, in turn, told him everything she had discovered about the Blackstone family in the old cemetery on the hill.

With the last of the orange-red sky giving way to dusk on the horizon behind him, Brad looked down at Sarah and smiled. "So tell me, Sarah, what exactly prompted you to come up here?"

"The Blackstone cemetery."

"That's just an excuse," he said. "What's your *reason* for coming up here?"

She lowered her eyes and nibbled on the strawberries. They were sweet and juicy and red, the perfect finish to a wonderful meal. Brad had said he had picked them that afternoon. These thoughts traveled vaguely through her mind as she calmly put aside his question. She had known him less than twenty-four hours. Why should she tell him?

But Brad didn't take any hint from her silence.

"You bicycled over a hundred miles all alone to see a cemetery where some Blackstones who may or may not be your ancestors are buried on land owned by two people you've never met." He popped several strawberries into his mouth, chewed them, and swallowed them while shaking his head knowingly. "There's got to be more to it than that. Why not drive? Why not at least take someone with you? Why go alone? For God's sake, why go at all?"

Sarah sprang to her feet, hoping to seem haughty and angry, not panicked, and tried to glare at him. He smiled smugly and ate three more strawberries. He knows he's gotten to me, she thought. "I figured it would be an adventure," she said inadequately.

He shook his head. "That's not all, Sarah."

"It's enough," she said levelly. "Any other reasons would require that you at least believe who I am."

Brad watched her turn her back to him and take her strawberries and coffee inside. His first impulse was to grab her and scoop her up into his arms so he could tell her it just didn't matter. He was intrigued by her, he wanted her, and he plain didn't care about who or what she purported to be. But he could see that more than what he believed and didn't believe disturbed her. He had pricked her most vulnerable point and, he guessed, most determined. She needed a few minutes alone. And, too, he knew what she would find in the living room.

Inside, Sarah sighed heavily and decided against going upstairs. She was too tired and full and not angry enough—not angry at all—to shut Brad out completely. She walked into the living room and began to regret storming out on him. How could he have known how sensitive she would be to those particular questions?

The cozy charm of the room instantly began to

work like a soothing balm on her tensed muscles. She paced in front of the chintz-covered couch and admired the exquisite patchwork of an antique quilt wall-hanging. Her eyes wandered to the long, narrow window that looked out onto the porch. She had to take only two steps to her left and she would see him. One foot lifted—

No! She planted it back on the floor and spun around, then stood rock-still. She was eye-to-eye with a blowup of a *New York Times* front page featuring a three-column photograph of a football player. She saw the grin first; then the laughing dark, dark eyes; the wet tousled hair; the dirty uniform.

"Oh, dear."

She didn't need to read the headline, but did anyway: NOVAS WIN SUPER BOWL. 31–14, and, in smaller print, 'MAGIC' CRAIG THROWS FOUR TOUCHDOWN PASSES.

Sarah grimaced. "Now I remember."

She could see herself at her desk on a damp Monday morning in late January reading *The New York Times* as she did religiously every morning. The Novas had just walked away with the Super Bowl championship. The article was before her then as it was now. Sarah hadn't watched the game, but, being a New Yorker, she had, of course, known the Novas were in the Super Bowl. She had even scanned the article.

Magic Craig. If he had introduced himself by his nickname, she *might* have remembered. Now, with that bold, charming, victorious face grinning and dripping with champagne in front of her, she remembered so very clearly. He hadn't lied. Brad was the Novas' quarterback.

"Not a bad picture, is it?" he said behind her.

Sarah turned and saw him leaning in the doorway. Her heart was beating furiously. This was Brad "Magic" Craig! *Oh, God, what have I gotten myself into. . . .*

He smiled languidly. "I wanted to win the Super Bowl just so my picture could be on the front page of the *Times*."

"I—I should have known who you were." She raked her fingers through her hair. It was all her brother's fault. He should have told her the people who had bought the old Blackstone estate were the parents of a football hero. He *had* to have known. Damn him! She hissed with irritation. "I should have known! I read that article and—and saw your picture six months ago. Your name sounded familiar, but I just couldn't believe—" She stopped herself and held out her hands helplessly, then let them flop to her sides. "You *are* Brad Craig."

He clicked his heels together and bowed.

Sarah groaned and flopped down on the couch. All his words flew back at her: *People have done stranger things to meet me. . . . A toss in the hay with me would play hell with your hamstrings. . . .*

"Oh, dear. Oh, damn." She propped her elbows on her knees and sank her face into her palms. "I'm stuck in the Catskills with a *football* player, an oversexed, swollen-headed *jock*!" She laughed almost giddily.

The sinking of the other end of the cushion warned her that Brad was beside her. She peered through her fingers and saw both long legs stretched out on the old worn pine coffee table. His casual shoes rested on top of the June issue of the *National Geographic*. He leaned back.

"I don't mind being called a jock," he said easily, knowing Sarah hadn't meant to be offensive, "but I think I'd prefer athlete. *Jock* has some rather unflattering connotations."

Sarah raised her face from her hands but didn't lean back. Her right thigh rubbed against Brad's pant leg, but to move it would only make him realize she had noticed. "I was only teasing you," she said. "I didn't mean to insult you, although you insulted me by assuming I engineered my entrance last night just to meet you. Brad, you may be a star quarterback, but I honestly didn't recognize you. Besides, I'm a Blackstone. If I had wanted to meet you, I assure you I would have done so without having to resort to such humiliating tactics."

He threw his head back against the couch and roared with laughter. Sarah automatically made a fist and belted him in the middle of his rock-hard stomach. Her hand came away very nearly bruised. "Stop laughing at me!"

He raised his head and looked down at her. "Scrappy little thing, aren't you?"

His mouth curled merrily, the dark eyes still laughing. He plucked her wrist up with two fingers. Her hand, which seemed so small next to his, was still clenched in a fist. "If you're going to make a fist, Sar, at least do it right. Tuck your thumb in—no, not *under* your fingers—right down there along the joints, almost into your palm." He took her hand fully into his and twisted her fingers so they made a proper fist. "If your thumb's on top or inside, you can break it just by hitting someone." He grinned. "Especially someone as hard as I am."

Sarah nodded. "I—I'll remember that."

His big hand lingered on hers and, whether or not he was aware of it, sent its warmth and calm up her arm and deep inside of her. "And if you're going to hit someone," he went on, "*hit* him." His hand moved up hers to her wrist. "Then run like crazy in case he decides to hit you back."

"I was just trying to get your attention."

His grin broadened as his hand closed around her wrist. "My point exactly. All you did was get my attention." He pulled her gently toward him, his eyes taunting, laughing. "Now you have to take the consequences."

"Brad, I don't *have* to take anything, you know," she said, amused. "I'm—"

"I know: You're a Blackstone," he finished for her, although that was not what she had intended to say. "And Blackstones don't have to put up with oversexed, swollen-headed jocks. Well, Sarah Blackstone, I'm a great big football player, and *I* don't have to put up with beautiful women belting me in the stomach." He grinned suddenly, his hand still holding her wrist. "We're acting like a couple of kids, aren't we? Fighting it out when you know I want to kiss you and I know you want me to kiss you. So—"

His grip loosened for the barest fraction of a second, and Sarah was up and on her way around the coffee table. "Wait a second!" Brad lunged and caught her by the hips and dragged her back down. "Good Lord, woman, tell me no if I'm wrong, but don't go scampering off like a frightened squirrel. You don't want me to kiss you?"

She had landed sprawled against him, his muscular arm anchored around her hips, her body squeezed between his long legs and that incredible arm. It was too much of an effort even to try to sit erect, curving her torso over his arm, so she fell back against his chest and laughed.

"Yes! Yes, I do want you to kiss me!" she admitted. "But I—"

That was all the encouragement he needed. He shifted so that she tumbled from his chest, but caught her around the shoulders with his other arm. She hadn't settled there when he brought his mouth to hers. There was no grin now, no merriment in those dark, dark eyes; only determination and longing as his lips tasted hers.

"Mmmm," he murmured between feathery kisses that tantalized her mouth and made her senses reel. "I wanted to do this all through dinner, Sarah, my love. I'd watch you lick these beautiful lips and think, 'My God, I could be there!'"

Sarah, my love. . . . It sounded so natural, spoken without the least hint of artifice or affectation, so *right.* "I—I had no idea."

Melting into his arms, she held back a cry for more of him as his lips treasured the corners of her mouth, gently baited the pliant flesh of her upper lip, pressed their moist softness to her full lower lip. Waiting for the kiss to deepen was agonizing, but she wouldn't have traded that moment for any other.

"You know us tough ballplayers," he said, chuckling, so close to her mouth that she could feel his warm breath, erotic in itself. Everything about him—every move, every muscle, every hair—made her want him more. "We're good at suppression."

She laughed throatily and he in turn felt her breath, warm and sensual, on his mouth. "You mean, you've watched a defensive tackle lick his lips and suppressed a desire to—"

Brad gave a low, incredulous growl at her daring tease. "All right, woman!"

Planting his feet flat on the coffee table and raising his knees, he rolled her against his chest, catching her head and neck against his left arm and cupping her under her bare knees with his right arm. Her skirt went awry, bunching halfway up her thighs. She was in his control now, pinned between his rock-hard chest and his rock-hard thighs, and suddenly she could think of nowhere she'd rather be. Nowhere on earth or in heaven.

"I need this," she whispered, her face tilted toward his, her eyes drinking in every nuance of the rugged planes of his face. "I need you."

Need! Oh, dear, had she spoken aloud? Had she said what the past twenty hours had branded in her heart! *I need you!* He didn't believe she was a Blackstone, so how could he understand all that she meant and all that those simple words had cost? They had seemed to come so easily, but they hadn't. Without the years of suffering, work, and sacrifice they might not have come at all. Six or seven years ago she might have seen Brad Craig and dismissed him as a jock and therefore inessential. Now she could not dismiss him at all. He was *there*. He was embedded in her consciousness, her subconscious, and she *did* need him. He was so warm and honest . . . so sensual. Just looking at him stirred her insides and made her crave his touch until she thought she might go mad.

Even with her blurred vision, she could see his thick scar lower ominously. Her breath stopped. "I'm not lying," she said in a voice thin from the absence of air in her lungs but full and steady from the honesty and conviction of her words.

Brad dropped his right arm so that her feet settled onto the cushion and then slowly, sensuously stroked the backs of her knees. He could see the truth in her eyes—and that strange, bewitching mix of vulnerability and determination. She seemed to have made up her mind that she would force him to believe her and yet seemed so afraid that he couldn't be forced and wouldn't believe. But how could he doubt the truth of her words?

She had lied about who she was, Brad told himself. Maybe that was the source of her vulnerability. She thought she needed to impress him and had made up that cock-and-bull story about being president of a corporation and chairman of a foundation. Now she had realized she didn't need to impress him. It was she and all she was that intrigued him, not the promise of wealth and titles. He still didn't know who she was, but in his heart he knew she wasn't one of those enticing, false women who liked to kiss and tell. There would be no articles from Sarah Blackstone exposing the life of the retired Magic Craig and their hours together.

Or would there be? He had been fooled before. The tender flesh behind her knees was as beguiling as the rest of her and made his blood pound, inflaming him with a desire he had never known before. Brad looked down at the slender body nestled against his, her breasts two soft, tempting mounds, the nipples like little buttons hidden beneath the stripes of her shirt. He wanted to touch her everywhere and never stop. She was so elegant and delicate, Brad thought, and yet so damn tough. *I just can't doubt her!*

"I know you're not lying," he said at last.

With his hand easing around to the tops of her knees, cupping them, he lowered his mouth and captured her sigh of relief with his lips. Her entire body seemed to smile and breathe into him. He could feel her own natural wariness begin to crumble. She was letting go. . . . Desire surged through him, but beyond that was a crying, demanding need not to hurt her. He was so used to dealing with women who expected—wanted—him to take from them and put nothing back. It was as if his finding sexual release with them was enough, something they could brag about in itself.

But Sarah was different, Brad realized. She seemed to be asking for all he could give, and offering all *she* could give in return.

He opened his mouth against hers and slowly ran his tongue across her lips, from one corner to the other, until he could feel her body shudder in response, wanting him, needing him as he so desperately wanted and needed her. Her lips parted for him, and his tongue plunged into her mouth, tasting every moist, dark corner.

He started to pull back, but her arms shot out and caught him around the shoulders and neck so that if he did pull back, she would go with him. His lips never left hers as his arms came around her, clasping her to him as he leaned back against the couch.

Her body stretched along his, on top of him, and Sarah shuddered with pleasure and awe at the hardness of the long body beneath her. She wanted to touch every inch of it and moaned with desire.

His mouth drew away from hers just long enough for him to breathe her name, but when he would have kissed her again, Sarah held back. She had to try to convince him one more time that she hadn't set him up. "Brad, I didn't mean for this to happen. I—it wasn't planned."

"I don't care!" he ground out. Then he smiled as he removed her glasses and set them on the side table. He smoothed her shining hair and repeated, quietly this time, "I don't care, Sarah."

His hands flowed down her shoulders, her waist, and he pressed his mouth to hers once again. With a sudden, powerful ache she felt the warmth and wetness of his tongue along the outline of her mouth. The ache swelled within her. Her mouth opened into his, and the heat of her tongue blended with his, deliciously scorching them both. She knew just where her body touched his, knew the depth of his arousal, knew how much she wanted this to go on and on.

When they drew apart, their breathing ragged with desire, Brad gently caressed the curve of her bare thighs and smiled. She smiled back. He moved to reclaim her mouth, but she was already sinking her head into his shoulder, feeling its hardness, the warmth of his cotton sweater, the intoxicating strength of his entire body. She tucked her hands under his arms, around his solid chest.

The ache within her was threatening to overwhelm all her senses. She didn't want to fight to control it. If she did, she didn't know if she would win. She didn't know if she wanted to win. And yet all she could feel, sense, was how hard Brad was, how strong and sensual, how much he wanted her . . . and how much she so very badly wanted him.

"I don't understand why—" Her words broke off

into a strangled sigh of longing and frustration. She would have fled then and there, but he held her tight, bringing his arms, so warm and re-assuring, securely around her.

"Sarah, Sarah," he said quietly, his lips just grazing the top of her head. "I want to love you. I can't tell you how much! We've known each other for such a short time. . . ."

He growled and cleared his throat, but before he could change his mind, he pulled her off him and sat her on the couch. She could feel his reluctance—his gallant sense of control—and respected him for it, because she knew she couldn't have expected the same of herself. They sat side by side, not touching.

Brad grinned down at her without apology or embarrassment. "That's one kiss I'll remember on cold winter nights," he teased, but there was a huskiness to his voice. *Damn,* he thought. *How much more can a man want a woman and still hold back?* "Well, at least you'll have a little something to tell your friends—"

Sarah leaped to her feet. "For the last time I am—" She stopped herself, hands on hips. "No, I won't say it again. You said I could drag out all my evidence as to who I am. Well, dammit, I will!"

"It's okay, Sar. I believe you're a Blackstone," he said calmly, amused now. He hadn't meant to set her off with his teasing: Was it a good sign he had? He smiled. "In fact, I think I've finally figured out who you are."

She groaned. "I can't wait. Tell me, Mr. Magic, who am I?"

He ran his thumb along his rugged jaw, thinking, Yes . . . that would explain just about everything! "A genealogist."

She groaned again, more loudly.

He clapped his hands onto his knees. "That's it, isn't it? I thought for a while you might be the penniless academic this rich Sarah Blackstone hired, but you said her name with too much gusto."

"Because it *is* my name."

"Exactly. Before I go on, Sar, how did you find out about this place?"

She crossed her arms on her breasts. "You won't believe me, so why should I tell you?"

He shrugged. "Okay. So what I figure is that there is no Blackstone Industries and no Blackstone Foundation. You made them up."

"And pray tell why?"

"To impress me." He grinned, enjoying himself now; enjoying her. "But I don't mind, Sar. I'm flattered. Anyway what I figure is you're a penniless genealogist—Sarah Blackstone—who decided to go out and research her own origins. As I said, you're creative."

"No, Brad, *you're* creative!" She spun on her heel and stalked toward the door.

"It's all right, Sarah," he called cheerfully, "I'd lots rather kiss a woman who's pretty and smart than one who's just rich."

"Will you stop teasing me!" She turned around and stomped one foot, more exasperated than angry. Brad's eyes twinkled merrily. "Dammit, Bradley Craig, I have more money than I'll ever be able to spend in a lifetime."

"Pretty, smart, *and* rich," he said laconically, the teasing disbelief undisguised. "My, my, it is my lucky week."

Even his teasing was sexy, curling up her spine, making her want to grin. She managed to huff and turn her back to him. Even if he was enjoying his "mystery" of figuring out who she might be, she couldn't deny what had happened between them a few minutes ago. Her body was still warm with the wonderful ache he had aroused within her. But he was so damnably *impossible*!

"Hey, aren't you going to help me with the dishes?"

She had started toward the center hall, but stopped in midstride. Leaving Brad with the dishes after he had cooked such a spectacular meal would be selfish and unfair.

"I'll do them myself," she announced without turning around. "You can stay in here and think about how infuriating you are. A penniless academic! A genealogist, for heaven's sake. Honestly, Brad."

"From your reaction, Sar, I'd say I hit the nail on the head. And of course, I'll help you with the dishes."

"No!" She hadn't meant to sound so panicked, but she couldn't imagine standing so close to him, washing and drying the stoneware, throwing accusations back and forth . . . ending up back in each other's arms. No, it wasn't that she *couldn't* imagine it; it was that she could imagine it only too well. She turned halfway around and smiled feebly. "I can manage on my own. I—I'd prefer it that way."

He shrugged, but he wasn't teasing her now. "Okay, Sarah, if that's what you want," he said, perfectly serious. He half smiled. "I hate doing dishes anyway."

"Well, then, we make a good team, because I hate to cook." She didn't catch herself anywhere near in time and only realized what she had insinuated when she was halfway across the living room. A team? She grimaced and felt the blush coming. "I mean—I didn't mean—"

She gave up before she could get herself in any deeper and fled, hearing Brad's rich laughter in the background. To her immense relief he didn't try to help her with the dishes, but respected her desire to do them alone. She hadn't touched a dishcloth in years, but she didn't mind the chore. The hot sudsy water and labor that demanded nothing from her mind and heart were almost therapeutic. She relished getting every plate sparkling clean, rinsing off the last bit of suds, washing Brad's knife and fork.

When she finished, she left the chicken pan soaking on the counter, gave the kitchen a proud look, and congratulated herself with a whimsical smile. She could hear the stereo playing softly in the living room, but she circled around and went down the hall, past Dorothy Craig's Hummels, to the center stairs. She didn't dare tempt herself further with the magical touch of Magic Craig.

And Brad remained motionless on the couch. He had put on music to drown out the clattering of dishes from the kitchen, or more specifically the presence of Sarah Blackstone. *I must be crazy*, he thought. But she seemed to belong in his life—and how long had it been? Not even twenty-four hours, hardly a day. And yet to fight against it seemed to be flying in the face of destiny.

Nuts! I don't know who the hell she is or what she's doing here.

If he saw her—if he touched her once more—he knew he wouldn't be able to stop himself . . . and she wouldn't want him to stop. *Destiny!* When he heard her tiptoe up the stairs, he kicked the *National Geographic* off the coffee table and growled fiercely. He didn't feel the least bit heroic for having resisted!

Five

The demons came in the night. She bolted up straight in her bed and stopped herself from screaming just in time. It was only a nightmare, *the* nightmare, but nothing more than a dream. The laughing, taunting false ghosts of father, uncle, and fiancé were the demons of her mind, distortions of the men she had loved. They had haunted her dreams for weeks after the tragedy, but she had banished them as she had adjusted to the reality of what had happened. Now they returned only occasionally, always unexpectedly, without apparent reason.

She trembled, more in anger than fear. The moon and stars were gleaming through the open window and cast eerie shadows. The demons were gone, but she knew sleep would elude her for a long time yet. She slipped out of bed and tiptoed downstairs, dressed only in her filmy nightgown.

Usually after the nightmare she would eat and watch late night television, but tonight she wanted to walk. She pushed open the back door and wandered outside into the night. The cool dew soaked her bare feet and the hem of her gown, but she paid no heed.

She stopped at the edge of the field above the house, at the stone wall surrounding the cemetery. The wind caught the white handkerchief-thin fabric of her gown and blew it around her legs. Goose

60

bumps rose on her arms. She didn't notice. She noticed only the names of her ancestors caught in the moonlight on the worn granite headstones.

Why had the nightmare, the demons, come back? *Dammit, why?* She folded her arms across her breasts and felt the fear and guilt creeping up her spine. Had they come because of Brad? Even now, standing in the cool night air beneath a half-moon, she could feel the warmth of his kisses and the ache of her arousal far more sharply than the terror of her nightmare.

She walked a few steps to the corner of the graveyard and stopped when she saw the moonlit headstone of Sarah Elizabeth Blackstone. She smiled with relief and felt the fear and guilt retreat. Of course! Her work in the cemetery—her discovery of her namesake's untimely death and that of her baby—had prompted the nightmare. The demons had come not because of Brad but in spite of him.

She turned away from the cemetery and started back, knowing the demons were gone for the night. They wouldn't be back . . . not for now, and with any luck not forever.

She didn't see the dark silhouette of a man in one of the upstairs windows. Brad had heard her footsteps and had automatically, intuitively, known she was going out into the night for a walk. But why? he asked himself. He saw her white figure on the lawn below. She seemed to float through the night. The moonlight caught her pale gleaming hair, her flowing white gown stood out against the darkness. She looked like a ghost, a nymph: a beautiful, wild, driven woman—delicate, determined, vulnerable.

His body went rigid when she paused in front of the cemetery, her gown swirling at her feet. Di finding that cemetery mean more to her than th names and dates of long-dead ancestors?

If something was bothering her, why didn't she come to *him*? He was there, he was alive, and he wanted Sarah as he'd never wanted a woman before.

When he heard her footsteps in the hall, only the most massive willpower kept him from going to her, taking her in his arms, and blotting out whatever it was that had sent her out into the darkness to an old and long-forgotten cemetery.

The next morning Brad found Sarah doing a charcoal rubbing of Sarah Elizabeth Blackstone's headstone. She had taped newsprint, which she had purchased in an early morning jaunt into the village, to the stone and was now carefully rubbing a smooth piece of charcoal along its contours to capture the lettering.

She had slept soundly after the late-night walk, and had awakened feeling more at peace with herself and her life than she had in a long time. She had resolutely pushed thoughts of Brad to the back of her mind, postponing having to deal with him and the aching need he created in her. Now every part of her body, every nerve ending, was aware of Brad's approach, aware that his magnificent body was only two feet behind her.

"Is she one of your foremothers?" he asked.

Sarah didn't look up—and tried to ignore her suddenly accelerated pulse. "Uh-huh."

"You're named after her?"

"After my great-grandmother, who was named after her great-grandmother—"

"Who's buried here?"

"Right."

"She died young, didn't she?"

Sarah nodded as her great-great-great-grandmother's dates, 1766–1800, came up on the newsprint. "Blackstones have a way of doing that."

She regretted her comment immediately. The morning was too warm, too glorious, to recall those horrible days of tragedy. To her relief Brad didn't ask her to. She chanced looking up at him and smiled. The sun glinted golden on his hair, and the worn jeans and T-shirt accentuated his muscularity. The mere sight of him instantly filled her with the longing she had felt in his arms the night before, but she quickly squelched it.

He studied her for a moment, as though questioning her without asking a question, and then he smiled. "I got a letter from my folks this morning, you know. They didn't mention any penniless academic that might show up on their doorstep."

"No? Nothing about a wealthy corporate president either?"

He grinned. "Not a word."

"Well, I'm sure they assume I received their message telling me their change in plans." She frowned at his skeptical, amused look. "How would you like to have your face smeared with charcoal, Mr. Magic?"

He merely laughed.

"Why, you big conceited ox!" But she was laughing as well. Her hands were covered with the chalky black stuff, so how could she possibly resist? She batted her eyes innocently as she climbed to her feet. "I suppose a 'little slip of a thing' like me ought to keep your superior strength in mind?" she asked in her best demure voice, which wasn't particularly convincing.

Seated on a rock with his arms folded across his chest and his legs stretched out, ankles crossed, Brad watched her with his mouth curved in amusement. "It would be wise."

She was standing next to his crossed ankles. "And of course, we penniless academics are known for our wisdom." She smiled coyly and edged her way up along those long, powerful legs. "Have you been sacked very often as a quarterback, Mr. Magic?"

"Often enough." He pursed his lips skeptically. "I thought you didn't know anything about football."

"Oh, I must have read it somewhere. You know we academics read everything." She was beside his thighs now. He was on a low rock, clearly not well balanced. One well-placed, well-timed shove . . . "Does it hurt when you get sacked?"

A slow grin crossed his face. "On the field usually, but I wear pads. Off the field . . ." He shrugged expansively, giving the term a double meaning Sarah hadn't considered.

His comment daunted her for a moment, but she refused to abandon her plan. "Tell me, Brad, have you ever been sacked by a woman—on the field, that is?"

"Nope."

"Oh, well, I was just curious, because I—"

She struck out with her blackened hands and lunged toward him in an attempt to throw him off balance and send him sprawling over the stone wall. Of course, he saw it coming. He grabbed her by the wrists before her hands touched his cheeks, and they both went over the wall. Sarah landed on top of him, but then her momentum carried her into a roll and she ended up alongside him in the grass. His grip on her wrists never wavered. He held her tightly and laughed.

"You're like a scrappy little banty chicken, Sar."

She was breathing hard, crushed against his long length, her wrists held out to her sides, safely away from his face. "I thought I was a bulldog."

"That too." He laughed again, his face and dark, dark eyes close to hers. "I'd love to kiss you, Sar, but I don't trust you with these hands."

"My hands?" she asked innocently. "Oh, of course, they're covered with charcoal. I forgot. . . ."

"Sarah," he warned. "Now, suppose you go wash up and meet me back out here. I've got a picnic basket filled with all kinds of goodies. I thought we could have a nice picnic up in the fields. I'll show you pictures of my new niece." He leaned toward her, still holding her wrists, and their noses almost touched. "And you can practice sacking me," he said with a devilish twinkle.

Before she could respond, Brad sat her and himself up, and then stood up with her. He finally released her wrists and turned her around. "Off you go."

Sarah considered trying again, but reminded herself that this man had quarterbacked the Super Bowl champions. More to the point, he hadn't been fooled the first time and therefore would hardly be fooled a second time. A verbal assault would have to suffice. She could at least have the last word.

"I'll get you yet, Brad Craig!" she called over her shoulder as she headed for the house, raising her arms above her head and wriggling her fingers.

Brad laughed. "Believe me, I can't wait."

At that moment she was grateful she had her back to him. So much for having the last word.

They decided to have their picnic beneath an old apple tree in the lush green field above the cemetery. Brad set the wicker hamper in the tall grass and dug out a red-checkered tablecloth. "What's a picnic without a red-checkered tablecloth?"

Sarah laughed and helped him spread the cloth in the shade of the tree. They anchored the corners with stones, then kicked off their shoes and plopped down together in the middle. Sarah lay on her back and stared up at the green leaves dancing against the blue of the sky.

"I've never taken a vacation in June before," she said happily. "It's a wonderful month. Everything's still so new and green. Tell me, do football players always get June off?"

Brad sat cross-legged beside her. "Usually we start getting geared up for training," he said.

"And are you gearing up?"

"No."

Something in his voice made her sit up beside him. He was frowning, but not at her. She waited for him to go on.

"I'm retired, Sarah. I figured the Super Bowl was a good note to quit on, so I did. I'm thirty-five years old, and I've had twenty good years of playing ball. That's enough." He cocked his head at her and half smiled. "I suppose you're going to tell me you didn't know?"

"Correct. I haven't had time to read the sports pages in years. . . ."

"Too busy prowling the library stacks?"

She didn't want to turn the conversation toward herself, so she ignored him. "What do you plan to do now?"

He shrugged. "I've had a few offers from corporations, but the thought of wearing a three-piece suit five days a week makes my skin crawl." He chuckled at the thought. "I've done a few commercials. I'm in demand right now because of those four lucky throws the third Sunday in January, so I'll probably cash in on my popularity and do a few more. Being a winning quarterback has its moments, Sarah. I get to do beer commercials and meet beautiful dripping-wet women who've lost their contacts in mud puddles—"

"My entrance and your being a quarterback are not related."

His "Right" told her he continued to have his doubts.

Sarah held back another denial and asked, "Do you have any other plans?"

"What? Doing beer commercials and tempting beautiful women isn't enough?" he teased. But his voice turned serious and he plucked at the hem of his jeans. "I'm considering a network offer to do announcing."

"That sounds like fun."

"Yeah, it could be," he said pensively. "Still, I'd like to do something beyond football with the second half of my life. . . ." His voice trailed off, but suddenly he grinned and quipped, "Maybe I could take lessons from a penniless genealogist on how to read a gravestone: 'Brad Craig, quarterback and ghoul—' "

"I am not a ghoul!"

He laughed.

Sarah groaned and shook her head, but it was only an act. She was happy and relaxed, more so than she had been in five long, long years. She lay down again on her back. "This trip isn't turning out at all as I expected."

"Thought I'd boot you out, didn't you?"

"I didn't know you existed, remember? What I meant— Well, never mind. It doesn't matter."

Brad stretched out beside her and propped his head up with one hand. "If not for my benefit, Sarah, why the lost contact and the hundred-mile trek?"

Looking into his eyes, she could see he wasn't teasing her now. She smiled whimsically and told him the truth. "I was trying to recapture the spirit and innocence of my youth, or some such thing."

His brow furrowed. "Why?"

Did he believe her? She shrugged at his question, although she knew the answer only too well. "I don't know. I'm turning thirty next month."

"So? I'm thirty-five."

"And you've never lost the spirit and innocence of your youth?"

"Well, maybe the innocence," he said, grinning. "It seems to me, Sarah," he went on, serious again, "that you've gone to pretty extraordinary lengths just to have some simple fun."

"Perhaps."

He smiled gently, with just a hint of teasing, and touched her chin with one finger. "Is the life of a penniless academic so dreary?"

"I wouldn't know," she replied coolly, but his smile was infectious, and she couldn't bite back her own smile. Nor could she ignore her reaction to his light touch.

"You've really become my mystery lady." He leaned toward her, his four fingers grazing the line of her jaw and easing down her throat. "I saw you outside last night, Sarah. At first I thought I was dreaming."

He paused, but she said nothing. She scarcely heard his words, concentrating instead on the heady warmth that flowed from his fingers through all of her body. She wanted to touch his hand, but held back, knowing that if she did, Brad would not stop as he had the night before. She had to be certain. . . .

"You looked like a ghost or a nymph out there, but then the moon lit on your hair. . . ." His voice, deep and melodic and sensuous, trailed off. His fingers never left the soft skin just below her jaw. "I haven't been able to shake that image of you, Sarah. You looked so haunted."

His fingertips brushed the pulse in her throat, quickening it. "I had a nightmare," she said. "It's of no importance now."

"You could have come to me," he said huskily. "You can come to me anytime, Sarah. I want to know more about you. I watched you last night and realized everything you've told me about yourself could be true, and it all could be a lie, but that it didn't matter. You're different from all the rest, Sarah."

She could sense how much he wanted to let go of his unnatural caution and cynicism, how much he wanted to drop that shield. "Not so different," she whispered. She at last covered the hand on her throat with her own, certain that Brad, for all he doubted her, was what she needed. "I want to touch you as much as all those women who have thought up ways to meet you. Brad. . . ."

Her lips parted in anticipation, inviting him, and he responded. His mouth covered hers, opened at once into hers, and their tongues shared a rising heat as they probed and tantalized every dark corner. Sarah moaned with a release of one tension and the sudden mounting of a new and exquisite tension deep inside her.

"Sarah, I want to make love to you," Brad said in a low voice as he carefully removed her glasses and set them out of harm's way. "I've wanted it since I saw you in that damn bathrobe, and I've been able to think of nothing else since I saw you out here last night like some Greek nymph. Sarah, Sarah!"

He kissed her again and again, and she could feel him struggling to control his desire and need. Did he want to be cautious and cynical? She welcomed his kisses and laid one hand on his lean, narrow hip. Her gentle touch was meant to tell him he could pull back if he needed to. He groaned, not hesitating, and rolled onto her, pressing her into the soft earth, seeking her mouth again. They kissed and tasted each other with the awareness that they wanted and needed the same thing.

His fingers grabbed at her shirt and pulled it from her jeans. "You could have put on a clean shirt, dammit," he muttered thickly. "You've managed to get charcoal all over me after all. I owe you one, Sarah Blackstone."

She laughed, but the soaring heat within her gave it a throaty quality.

The shirt came free, and Brad pushed it up her stomach and over her head, then cast it aside in the grass. "Ah," he murmured in appreciation, placing a palm above her breasts. He ran a teasing finger down between them and gently unsnapped the middle of her front-wrap bra. "I was wondering which one of these you'd be wearing. I see you don't go for wires—"

"I don't exactly need the support," she said wryly.

He ran his finger across the rounded peaks of her breasts and opened his eyes wide in mock astonishment when the nipples hardened beneath the filmy fabric.

"Well," he said hoarsely, "you don't need padding either."

A breeze blew across the field, further enticing her nipples. Brad quickly dispensed with the bra, shrugging it off her rounded shoulders and tossing it aside with the shirt. When he returned to her, he placed a hand on either side of her shoulders and held himself above her. He gazed down at her.

"You're so beautiful, Sarah," he said simply.

She smiled with pleasure, but when he made a move to kiss her again she held up a hand. "Brad, before we go any further, there's something you should know. I didn't bicycle up here with anything like this in mind—no matter what you think—and so I'm not protected."

"Another clue for my mystery," he muttered. "But not to worry now." He nodded toward the wicker hamper. "You can just imagine all the goodies I packed, Sarah."

"You mean . . . ?" She met his eyes and laughed. "Never underestimate a man of your . . . stature."

He touched her then, and all thought of teasing went out of her mind. His lips pressed against hers, then against her chin, her throat, and in whispery little kisses across the soft flesh of her breasts. Sarah held back, not touching him, until he seized the hardness of a nipple between his lips, and then captured it gently in his teeth.

Her hands coursed through his thick hair. She could feel only her need for him, the white heat of his kisses, the swelling ache of her desire. His hands caught her about the hips, his fingers pressing into the lean flesh there, and slowly his mouth descended along the tautness of her stomach.

And then in a blinding flash they were touching each other everywhere. They tugged at the last, remaining barriers to their passion. Brad's shirt went first, revealing the well-developed muscles and thick dark hairs of his chest and shoulders. Sarah paused to drink in the sight of him, but already Brad was pulling at the belt on her jeans.

"Do you know how many times I've wondered what it would be like to run my hands along your chest?" she murmured. "Oh, Brad, I want to touch you."

"You will, darling, you will."

The belt went, then the jeans, then her underpants—the blue ones with the lacy trim, but he didn't comment on them. He tried to pause to gaze at her, but her fingers, trembling with passion, sought out his belt.

In a moment they were naked to each other's desire.

The touching and tugging didn't stop. Sarah felt as though she were touching a man, and being touched, for the first time in her life. No part of her was free from Brad's passionate kisses or the skillful probing and feathery touches of his hands. She couldn't get enough of him even as she ran her hands along every hard muscle.

"Sarah, Sarah, I want you so much! I can't wait any longer—"

He drew her fully against him, wrapping his legs around her so that she could feel his throbbing desire against her. "Neither can I," she moaned breathlessly.

He rolled onto his back, taking her on top of him, and reached one long arm out toward the picnic basket. He smiled into her eyes as he flipped the lid and rummaged inside. "Ah-ha!" Sarah made a move to roll onto her back, but he held her where she was. He looked at her gently. "It's been awhile for you, hasn't it?"

She nodded truthfully, not embarrassed by his question, his concern.

He smiled with understanding. "It'll be good, Sarah," he whispered and, with her slightly to one side, swiftly and deftly prepared himself. "I don't think—" He hesitated, as if wondering if he should go on, but when Sarah looked into his eyes, baring her soul, he touched the softness of her shoulder and said, "I don't think I've ever wanted a woman the way I want you."

"Brad—"

Her mouth lowered to his, and they kissed tenderly, holding back the heat of their passion for a few gentle seconds. Then Brad cupped her hips in his hands—she could feel their calluses—and she arched above him. In that fiery instant, they were consumed by each other, and then one into the other.

Nothing could hold them back now. Sarah moved; he answered. Every movement was as if they were one. She knew only the thrusts of his body within her, and of the responding heat of her body within him. Nothing else was; nothing else mattered.

"Brad!" she gasped, and pulled herself flat against him. "Oh, Brad!"

Then she felt the breeze on her back and smelled the freshness of the air and the sweetness of the field as if for the first time; as if she had never smelled anything so fresh nor so sweet. She smiled down at the man beneath her. Could she have fallen in love in two short days? He smiled back, and she knew that that smile, that strong, friendly face, that dark hair—all of him would be etched in her memory forever.

She rolled onto the cloth beside him as the breeze cooled their overheated bodies. "Oh, Sarah," he said, the richness of his voice giving untold depth and meaning to the simple words.

Perspiration glistened on his strong, perfectly conditioned body, giving Sarah an odd but undeniable sense of pleasure. Their passion had made that incredible body sweat! She pressed her thumb to his chest and flicked away a salty drop. He captured her hand in one of his, brought it to his lips, and kissed each of her fingers lingeringly. Sarah turned onto her side and snuggled close to Brad, laying her head on his shoulder. His arm wrapped around her and he hugged her.

"Sarah," he said, not a hint of teasing in his voice, "you know I'm no innocent little boy."

She stirred restlessly, but he only held her more tightly.

"I've had more women throw themselves at me, offer themselves to me, but never"—he nuzzled her hair—"never have I felt like this."

"How do you feel?" she asked softly after a moment's pause.

Brad shifted, rolling Sarah onto her back so he could see her face. "I don't think the words exist to describe how I feel. I've just never felt so close, so . . . so . . . right with another woman—another person—before."

Sarah stroked his face gently with a trembling hand. "Neither have I," she whispered. Her hand trailed down to his neck, then to his still damp chest. She smiled teasingly. "You sure worked up a sweat, though."

His eyes twinkled. "I haven't had such a good workout in weeks, Sar."

She chuckled, watching her fingertips run down his chest and across the ripples of steel of his stomach, intrigued and awed by this man who had so easily and so completely filled her body and soul. New York and her responsibilities there seemed far, far away. Then she thought of all the responsibilities Brad must have given up after winning the Super Bowl. "Do you miss it?" she asked quietly.

"Darling," he said, refusing to be serious, "I'd rather exercise with you than bench-press a hundred and fifty pounds—"

"I don't weigh a hundred and fifty pounds!"

His rich, hearty laugh echoed across the fields and brought little shivers to the base of Sarah's spine. "Sorry, that's not exactly what I meant," he said, unabashed.

She laughed and felt the twinkle in her own eyes. Had she ever been this free in her near thirty years? "And *I* was talking about football—do you miss it?"

He crooked his elbow, propped his head up in one hand, and considered her question as his free hand idly traced circles on her bare shoulder. "I love football, and I loved playing," he replied. "But that part of my life is over—the playing part at least. I see myself as moving on, more than giving up something. I've always had a full, rounded life, Sarah, and I continue to go on having one."

"You've never had trouble mixing work and play, keeping Magic Craig the all-star quarterback in perspective with Brad Craig the man?"

She's so serious, Brad thought, seeing the curiosity—and the determination—in her beautiful pale green eyes, but her interest and her sensitivity to the dual life he sometimes led, to who and what he had been and was, enticed him. She seemed to understand. She seemed to empathize, as though she had been there before. But how could she have experienced it? Unless . . . no, it couldn't be. He was *sure* the foundation and the company were amusing figments of her imagination.

"It hasn't always been easy," he admitted. "The demands of being a quarterback can be pretty intrusive at times—not only on my time, but on *me*." But she knew that, didn't she? *That* wasn't what she wanted to know! He shook off his confusion. "Sometimes I thought I'd lose sight of who Brad Craig is and what he wants out of life."

"And did you?"

It wasn't an idle question and suddenly Brad realized that this was what she wanted to know. *Why?* "No, not really," he said, almost matter-of-factly. "When I realized what was happening, I'd pull back—quit partying and giving interviews, even reading stuff people wrote about me, and go up into the mountains or just hide out in my apartment with my headphones on, listening to records. I'd do whatever it took to get back onto an even keel."

She nodded as if she understood—as if she envied him, in a way—and laid her hand gently on the tautness of his hip. He could feel her fingers splayed against his brown skin and knew they belonged there. This was the touch, the woman, he'd been waiting for all his life. Her eyes searched his. "Are you here in the Catskills because you're pulling back, Brad?"

His eyes narrowed thoughtfully as he remembered the questions of another woman, another time: *Are you here in the mountains because you're thinking of retiring? Are you afraid to retire? What do you plan to do with the rest of your life?* He had trusted her enough to have her meet him in the mountains for a day, but her questions had made him suspicious. He remembered the panicked look on her face when he had calmly dug her wallet out of her bag and found the press pass. She didn't need any help packing her bags!

He hated being taken for a fool . . . and worse, *being* one. Hard lessons had taught him to be cautious. But when his eyes searched Sarah's and he saw no guile, when he felt the gentle pressure of her fingers on his flesh, when his maleness stirred with passion and love, he knew he had to take the chance. She was worth it. They—what they were and could be together—were worth it.

"In a way yes," he said at last. "I've got the rest of my life to consider. I want to make the right decisions. My parents needed someone to look after the place while they were gone, so I took the opportunity to do some thinking."

"I hope I'm not intruding—"

"Sarah, Sarah, Sarah," he said, touching her hair, laughing low and lovingly. "This seemed as good a place as any to go to, but I have a feeling it was destined—"

"I know just what you mean," she interrupted with an enthusiasm and excitement that made her seem so young, so vulnerable, that Brad marveled at how a moment ago she could have been so determined. What a wonderful, fascinating woman! She smiled at him, her half-blind eyes shining. "You know, Brad, I swear if I'd decided to get my act together and my life into some kind of livable balance by climbing Mount Everest, I'd have found you waiting at the top with one of your big sexy grins on your face."

Brad rolled onto his back and laughed at the sky, then turned back to Sarah with a mischievous gleam in his dark, dark eyes. "You'll never guess what, Sar," he said, brushing his knuckles across her collarbone, then her soft breasts, watching in delight as the two buttonlike nipples rose up, "but if my sister hadn't gone into labor prematurely, I probably would have gone off to climb Mount Everest. . . ."

"Oooh, Brad!"

She snorted in disbelief and playfully shoved his shoulder, but he caught her about the waist and pulled him to her. His mouth found hers with such hunger that Sarah's laugh was abruptly cut off and she could only wrap her arms around his steely nakedness and bring herself to him.

"Think if we'd had to make love on top of

Everest," he murmured between plundering kisses. Finally he eased himself on top of her, his weight giving her warmth and pleasure, driving her wild with mounting desire. "I think I'll die if I don't have you again," he breathed into her ear, then wet it sensuously with his hot tongue.

They made love with an urgency that almost made Sarah's breath stop. Brad not only gave but took from her, demanding from her the same emotional and physical response he gave to her. Even if she had wanted to, Sarah couldn't have denied him. Even deep within the frenzy of their passion, with his body pulsing inside her, she knew he was giving all of himself . . . and expecting all of herself in return. If she could have fooled herself before, she couldn't now; this was no "toss in the hay" for Brad "Magic" Craig.

He wrapped his arms around her, crushing her to him, and that moment of release—of pulsating, wondrous ecstasy—seemed to go on forever. Sarah was aware only of the blinding fervor of her passion, and of his, and of how perfectly it was being quenched deep, deep inside her.

Six

They picnicked and laughed and looked at pictures of the new baby. Afterward they shook out the cloth and collapsed, the tall grass tickling their toes.

Sarah awoke in a half-asleep, nightmarish panic

and gazed at the long, slumbering form beside her.

Who is this man? My God, have I created him, or is he real? I've known him such a short time and yet it feels like forever, and life can't go on without him and . . .

Why am I so afraid?

"Oh, dear, what have I done?" Sarah whispered.

My work and my responsibilities—my life—are all back in New York. My mother, Aunt Anna, my cousins, Hamilton, the people who work for Blackstone Industries—they all depend on me. They trust me! And I've been making love under an apple tree to the most wonderful man in the world!

"And he thinks I'm a penniless academic."

She wiped the sweat of panic and confusion from her brow and listened to the steady rhythm of Brad's breathing. Had destiny brought them together or had her crying need for *him*—not just someone like him, but *him*—forced her to create him? Was she seeing him not as he was but as she wanted him to be? And even if she was, she was being unfair and presumptuous. When she had rationally and coldly examined her life and decided she didn't like the direction in which it was going, she had realized that change was up to her. She had come to the Catskills alone because she had decided that the change that must occur was within herself. No one could change her life for her. She had to do it alone! Who said Brad wanted to help her? Who said he *could* help her?

She had to leave. She blew him a parting kiss and within ten minutes had gathered up her belongings, scrawled him a note, and was gone, pedaling down the country road on the first miles of her long journey to Manhattan.

She was sailing down a hill in tenth gear when a sleek black Lotus Elite slowed beside her and matched her speed. She shot the driver an annoyed glance, but her eyes riveted on the tousled dark hair and angry glare of Brad Craig.

"Oh, dear."

She squeezed the handle brakes and didn't realize her feet had dropped down until they tangled up in the pedals. She tore her gaze from Brad, but it was already too late. As she pressed hard on the brakes, that the bike salesman had bragged could stop on a dime, she came to an abrupt and ungraceful halt on the long steep hill.

The pedals spun wildly, whipping her ankles, and before she could cry out she was tumbling onto the sandy shoulder of the road. She would have rolled several yards, but the bicycle had hold of her legs and a pedal dug unmercifully into the ankle caught on the bottom.

"Damn you, Bradley Craig!"

Outrage dulled the pain as Sarah propped herself up and slipped her nylon pack off her back. The Lotus had stopped a few yards down the road. She glowered at it and slowly lifted her left leg from the top of the fallen Raleigh. Everything was intact, if bruised. She wasn't sure about the other leg. Normally not one to curse, she cursed. She was sitting up awkwardly now, trying to free her right leg from her vehicle without doing further damage to either herself or her bike.

A dark shadow fell over her, and she glared up at Brad. He stood ramrod-straight and looked down at her.

"Don't think I'm worried," she snapped. "I'm a hell of a lot madder than you are. You could help me, you know!"

His eyes narrowed. "Have you ever considered taking a bus?" he asked sardonically. "You and your damn bicycle."

"Brad, please!"

He obviously wasn't amused. The stiffness of his spine and the unsympathetic twist of his jaw told her that much, not to mention the way he hadn't leaped to her aid. Sarah wrestled with the bike herself, but when she pulled the handlebars up, the pedal dug more deeply into her anklebone. She let out a yell.

"Well, it serves you right," he muttered.

"It does not!"

He grabbed the bike by the fender and handlebars and jerked it upward. Sarah yelled again and quickly twisted her leg, pulling her ankle free before it could be further mangled. "Ow, ow, ow! *Damn it*, Brad, couldn't you go a little easy?"

Brad set the bike upright, gave the kickstand a little more kick than it needed, and squatted down in front of Sarah. She sat in the sand with the merely bruised leg stretched out, its knee bracing her injured ankle. It hurt too much for her to do anything more than curse it and Brad.

"Let's see," he ordered.

She raised her eyes to him. "Go away. I don't need Attila the Hun looking after me."

His eyes opened slightly wider and almost twinkled, but he caught himself in time and looked back down at the ankle. He grabbed her shin and tugged off her sneaker.

"Ow!"

"Don't be a coward."

"I'm not being a coward. If I were being a coward, I'd be rolling around screaming and writhing in pain. Ouch! Brad, will you please be careful? No, not the sock!"

"Quit grumbling.

"You're a jock. You're used to pain." She grimaced when he pulled off the sock, not at all gently, but refused to yell. She cursed instead.

"The best way," he said, dropping the sock into the sand, "is the quickest way."

"And where did you get your medical degree?"

"I just know that from twenty years of being knocked around on a football field." He propped the ankle on his knee and looked at it. "You've got a pretty good scrape here."

"Scrape? That's a *gash*."

"You're exaggerating."

"Scrapes don't bleed."

He shrugged. "Okay, you've got something between a scrape and a gash—" he turned the ankle slightly—"and one hell of a good bruise."

She put both hands out flat behind her and leaned her weight on them. "Is there anything broken?"

He looked straight into her eyes. "Not yet."

She swallowed.

"I can drive you back to the house so you can get patched up."

"I'll be all right."

He stood up abruptly, dumping her ankle onto the sand shoulder. "I ought to wring your little fool neck, Sarah."

"My neck is not little or fool, and you have no business wanting to wring it!" She raised her knees and tilted her head back to look up at him. She felt the blood oozing from her ankle, but knew it would be all right. More than the pain, she felt Brad's anger and her own. "If anyone deserves a wrung neck, it's you! What did you think you were doing sneaking up on me like that?"

"How the devil can a car sneak up on a bicycle?"

"You would drive one of those quiet sneaky little cars!" She sat up straight, momentarily forgetting which ankle hurt more. Brad stood in front of her like a panther ready to spring. "If it hadn't been for you— Dammit, why didn't you catch up with me at the bottom of the hill or at least *honk*? No, honking would have been worse."

"You're lucky I didn't just run your little ass over!" He growled furiously, whether at himself or her Sarah wasn't sure, and turned away. "And don't talk to me about sneaking, Sarah Blackstone."

She hobbled to her feet and balanced herself unsteadily on her left leg. "I didn't sneak off, Brad, I—I stole away." She licked her lips. It was a fine distinction at best, and a poor excuse. "You're right, I am a coward."

He didn't turn to her. "That was one hell of a note you left me, Sar: 'To be fair to you, I have to leave. I'll be in touch. Sarah.' God! I was so damn mad, I ripped the thing to shreds and came after you." He turned to her now, his eyes hooded with frustration, his fists clenched and massive at his sides. "Did you really think you'd get enough distance between you and me on that damn bike of yours?"

"Well, no, I—" She paused. Her leg was getting tired, her ankle was throbbing, and all her resolve and sense of purpose of an hour ago was weakening. Why had she left? "I didn't really think you'd follow me."

He grunted. "For an academic, Sar, you aren't very smart about some things." His voice lowered, softening, but there was still a rough edge to it. "Why did you leave?"

His eyes held hers, refusing to let her go, and although he didn't touch her, she couldn't tear herself away from that penetrating gaze. "Because I had to," she said. "Because you won't believe who I am, because I am who I am, because what we have between us has happened so fast, maybe too fast, because it isn't real in the sense—"

"You felt pretty damn real to me, Sarah."

"In the sense that it could have or would have happened anywhere else, any other time." At last, free of his gaze, she looked away. "Maybe that doesn't make a great deal of sense to you, but it does to me. My life isn't entirely my own, Brad. I want it to be and it *will* be, but—"

His fists opened and closed at his sides, his powerful arms tensed. "You'll have to do a hell of a lot better than that, Sarah," he said darkly. "That's just not good enough. Dammit, woman, I held you in my arms just a few hours ago! And now you're telling me you snuck off because of who you are and—" He stopped, and his eyes held her just as surely as the hard muscles of his arms would have. His voice dropped ominously. "Who are you, Sarah Blackstone?"

"I've *told* you: I'm chairman of the board of—"

"Don't give me that line again!" He kicked the sand with his toe, sending up a shower of tiny rocks and dirt. "You've been smart and awfully damn creative from the very beginning, but to my eternal damnation I *believed* you." His eyes held hers once again, piercing her; his nostrils flared with angry breaths. "What's setting me up been worth to you, Sarah? Just a toss in the hay—or more?"

She stared at him. "Haven't you been *listening*?"

"Yeah." He spun around and stalked toward the car. "Have a good bike ride, Sar."

"Brad!"

He climbed into the car.

"Brad, my ankle—how am I going to bicycle all the way to New York?"

"Call your chauffeur." He slammed the door shut.

Sarah watched in helpless fury as he started the Lotus and drove away. When she got to Manhattan, her first act would be to mail that conceited lummox a copy of the Blackstone Foundation annual report! She plopped down in the sand. Her ankle had stopped bleeding, but she doubted that it and her bruised leg were up to pedaling. She supposed she *could* call her chauffeur—her mother's in any case. A smile crept up on her. Brad Craig had come after her—*he* had pursued her—and yet he still didn't believe she was the wealthy Sarah Blackstone. Whatever attracted her to him, it wasn't her money!

A mile down the road the Lotus Elite slid to a silent halt. "What the hell," Brad muttered and huffed in exasperation. "Dammit, who is she?" A corporate president? A penniless academic? A woman who had wanted to meet him and thought up a good story to worm her way into his life and now couldn't get herself out of her lie? A hired sneak—*whose?*—assigned to find out what Brad Craig planned to do now that there were no more "next seasons" and now that she had given herself to him—she couldn't deny that!—didn't know how to face him with the truth? *Did it matter?* Brad growled in frustration and turned the car around. "What the hell."

She was still smiling and watching her ankle swell when the black sports car slid to a stop beside her. Brad's lithe, lean, powerful figure climbed out of the car, and Sarah had to fight back an urge to throw her arms around him, to apologize and ask him if she could change her mind—if she could stay. But she *had* to leave the Catskills. She had to!

He stood beside her with his hands on his narrow hips. "The least I can do is see you safely to the bus."

His deep, earthy voice made her breathless, but she spoke calmly. "Okay, but my bike won't fit in your car. What about it?"

"Collateral," he said, his eyes menacing. "You can get it back when you return."

Then he did want her to return! she realized. Sarah smiled. "I can afford to buy another, you know."

"Right."

"It's true." She hobbled to the car and fell onto the seat. "Does that mean you want me to come back?"

He grabbed her pack and dumped it onto the floor at her feet, just missing her injured ankle. "Maybe."

"Because if it does," she went on fearlessly, "you don't need the bike as collateral. All those bones and muscles and sinews of yours will suffice."

The thick scar above his eye went up.

She gave him a self-satisfied smirk. "Don't worry, I didn't learn to talk like that from the Blackstone women. They'd be horrified."

He shifted the car into first and sped off.

"Wait, my bike's out in the open—"

"You can afford another, remember?"

"Yes, but it's a perfectly good bike!"

He smiled sardonically. "And I'm sure whoever ends up with it will appreciate it."

"But, Brad!"

He glanced at her. "Yes?"

"The Blackstone family didn't get rich by leaving things for thieves," she muttered. "You'll go back for it, won't you?"

A pleasant, sexy smile broke across that strong face. Sarah longed to touch him. No one had ever smiled like that at her, she thought. It made her breath go short; reached inside and touched her heart; made her want to close her eyes and remember what making love to him on his red-checkered tablecloth in the shade of the apple tree had been like.

"Maybe," he said curtly, but with an undertone of amusement. "I figure you'll come back just to find out for sure. You can't resist a mystery any more than I can."

She refused to comment, but looked out at the green, mountainous countryside. She *had* to leave. If only she could avoid looking at him for a few more miles. . . .

When they reached the bus station, she put on her stocking and discovered her ankle had swelled so badly, it barely fit into her shoe.

"It'll be fine," Brad promised. "I used to wake up with ankles like that every other morning. Have enough money for the bus?"

She groaned. "Yes!"

Brad flashed the tantalizing grin; his eyes were laughing. "Just checking."

She pushed open the door and winced at the dull pain emanating from her shoulder. Was it bruised too? "Well, I'll have plenty to remember you by."

"I should hope so." He laughed. "You're blushing, Sar."

"Exertion," she corrected, but smiled. "I hope one day you'll understand why I'm leaving. I—I'll be back for my bike."

"Right." Letting her go was so damn hard! But again Brad could sense that mixture of determination and vulnerability, which he was no closer to understanding, and knew that she needed to pull back and that he had to let her go . . . for now. He *would* find out who she was! He grinned at her and winked. "So long, mystery lady."

She held up a hand tentatively, uncertain now just how irrevocable her decision was. If he asked her to stay . . . "Good-bye, Brad."

He didn't ask her to stay. When she shut the door, he winked a final time, smiled, and drove off— and she had no idea what that wink and smile had cost. Sarah watched the Lotus disappear around a corner before she hobbled into the bus station.

"You're a nitwit," she muttered aloud.

But as she purchased a ticket for New York she knew she would be back for her Raleigh ten-speed . . . and her quarterback.

If, that is, he still would want her when he learned she was far, far from being a penniless academic.

Twenty-four hours later Brad was sitting on the front porch idly unfolding a letter neatly typed on heavy rag stationery. How much time, he wondered, would he be willing to give Sarah before swooping back into her life? Damn, he didn't even know where she lived! It didn't matter; he'd find her. He hissed impatiently and lowered his gaze to the letter.

He focused on the understated gold-embossed lettering at the top: BLACKSTONE INDUSTRIES, INC. In smaller black lettering was its East 50th Street address and a listing of its officers: Hamilton Blackstone IV, chairman of the board; Sarah Blackstone, president and acting chief executive officer; and Corbin Delaney, executive vice-president.

"Well, I'll be damned!"

Either she hadn't lied at all, or her lie extended to creating a very convincing letterhead. Whatever, Brad couldn't stifle a deep, rumbling chuckle. What a fun, amazing woman!

Still chuckling, he glanced at the letter, but when he saw the signature, his laughter stopped short. He had expected some arrogant scrawl from Sarah Blackstone, but what he saw was the neat, haughty penmanship of Hamilton Blackstone IV. "What the hell?" He read on:

Dear Mr. Craig:

As chairman of the board of Blackstone Industries and a trustee of the Blackstone Foundation, I cordially invite you to attend the meeting of the Board of Trustees of the Blackstone Foundation next Thursday morning, June 28, at ten o'clock. I would like very much to take that opportunity to introduce you to the other trustees, myself included, and to acquaint you with the programs of the foundation. We are most interested in having you join us in our work. I know this letter must come as a surprise and I apologize for the short notice, but I do hope your schedule will permit you to join us on Thursday.

With every good wish

Sincerely,

Hamilton Blackstone IV
CHAIRMAN OF THE BOARD

Brad shook his head. "Hell's bells." Until Sunday night when Sarah had whipped his robe around her slender body and rattled off her titles, Brad had never heard of Blackstone Industries or the Blackstone Foundation. Now this! The tone of the letter—and its brevity—intimated that any living, breathing citizen of the United States *should* have heard of them.

"No, uh-uh!" Brad thwacked the letter. "She made this H.B. the Fourth up too! The little conniver . . ."

H.B. . . . Hamilton Blackstone . . . Ham . . . "No, it couldn't be." Brad muttered, frowning deeply.

He leaped off the porch and in long, easy strides ran to the old Blackstone cemetery. The headstones twinkled in the sun as if they were laughing at him—or with him, he thought grimly; time would tell which. He counted off five Hamilton Blackstones, two having died in infancy. His frown deepened. *Nuts! I must be crazy. . . .*

He took the same long, easy strides back to the house and grabbed the phone in the kitchen, punching out a number he knew so well. He asked for Ham Black, but his buddy and trainer wasn't around. "Give him a message for me, okay?" he ground out. "Tell him if Ham Black is also Hamilton Blackstone the Fourth—or if he's even *heard* of this guy—he's dead meat. Got it?" The message-taker said yes and nervously asked if he was serious; Brad grunted. "Maybe."

It all depended, he thought, when he'd hung up, on one hell of a lot of whys and wherefores. Number one: Was the woman he had held in his arms yesterday—and wanted even now—exactly who she had claimed she was all along? If so, what did that make Novas' trainer Ham Black? Ham was no damn corporate chairman! Brad growled in frustration. How the hell could the chairman of the board of a corporation end up as a football trainer? And Ham had been his closest friend for the past year. Surely he wouldn't have deceived Brad like this, would have told him . . .

But what if Ham had deceived him? Did Sarah know? Dammit, she had to! Her midnight appearance had to have been an act, something she and her brother had cooked up. . . .

But *why*? If she had wanted to meet Magic Craig, Ham could easily have arranged it. In fact, he remembered Ham saying a number of times that Brad ought to meet his sister. So why all the theatrics?

And what the hell was this letter about? Was the past few days nothing more than a lure to get Brad Craig, football star, to sit on the board of trustees of the Blackstone Foundation? That was absurd!

No. The simplest, most logical explanation was that Ham Black was Ham Black and nothing more, and that he and his beautiful sister—a couple of reckless nuts—had cooked up an elaborate practical joke to play on one retired quarterback.

But he was on to them now—*and* he'd have his revenge. He thwacked the letter again and began to laugh. Where the hell had those two come up with such a nutty idea? He considered calling back the Novas' office and canceling his message, but decided against it. "Ha! Let the little schemers roast awhile."

He thought of Sarah—missing her, wanting her—and saw the image of her floating across the lawn with the moon on her pale hair . . . with that mixture of determination and vulnerability. Had the practical joke gotten out of hand? "Oh, Sarah, Sarah," he murmured huskily, "I'll give you a few days but no more. Then I'm coming after you, sweetheart! And we'll see—oh, yes, dear heart, we'll see."

Seven

The following Monday morning Sarah returned to her office and her duties with the feeling she was sinking into a deep hole and never would be able to crawl out again and see the sun. Even the Tiffany furnishings and Persian carpets of her plush East 50th Street office failed to rouse her to the spirit of being a Blackstone. She stuck her tongue out at the proud portrait of Hamilton Blackstone, Sr., that hung above the massive desk . . . his desk. She had his fair hair and pale green eyes, but she doubted the man who had founded Blackstone Industries and the Blackstone Foundation and made the first Blackstone million a hundred years ago had had dimples . . . or had ever made love in the shade of an apple tree.

And yet she *was* proud to be a Blackstone, to have that man in the portrait in her family tree. Tragedy had twisted the plans she had had for her life. She had never expected to become president of the family company and chairman of the family foundation at age twenty-five, but what choice had there been? And last year when her brother had decided to take a leave of absence from his position as chief executive officer, what choice had she had but to step into his shoes?

She glowered at the portrait and sighed wearily. She had too many responsibilities—or was it too many dreams? And no choice. No choice at all.

She knew—and accepted—her duty to her family, to her mother and aunt and cousins, to future generations of Blackstones, even to the dead Blackstones—her father and uncle and the old codger in the portrait.

She knew they weren't the reason for her sinking feeling. Mr. Bradley "Magic" Craig was. For five days while visiting friends and trying to relax, she had thought about him almost constantly and cursed him and half hoped he would come after her. She debated driving back to the Catskills and picking up where they had left off.

And where had they left off?

Sar the mystery lady . . . the genealogist . . . the little slip of a thing . . . the banty chicken . . . the little bulldog . . . the penniless academic.

No conversation with her friends, no book, no television program or movie, no amount of walking on the quiet beaches of Long Island, could distract her. She had thought only of Brad and all that he had come to mean to her in so short a time. Now she could scarcely concentrate on her work or even think about her enormous responsibilities. How could she become so *obsessed* with a man in *two days*?

There was a gentle rapping on the door, and Sarah composed herself. At her calm "Come in," her svelte, dark-haired secretary, Debbi Josephs, entered. "Excuse me, Ms. Blackstone, but I thought you'd want to know that a man in the outer office is demanding to see you. I know you asked not to be disturbed this morning, but he's giving the receptionist a hard time."

Sarah sighed. Welcome back to work, she thought. "Have you called security?"

Debbi scratched her nose, hesitating. "Well, I'm not sure how much good it would do, and the publicity—"

A scuffle in Debbi's office, beyond the open door, interrupted her. They heard the panicked, high-pitched voice of the receptionist. "I don't care *who* you are! I *cannot* allow you in! Ms. Blackstone asked not to be disturbed."

The reply was deep, patient, and to the point. "Tough."

Debbi licked her lips nervously and Sarah felt her face grow pale. It sounded like . . . it could be . . . Her earlier depression vanished. The receptionist's matronly figure appeared in the doorway, and she blocked the intruder's path by putting one hand on either side of the frame. The hearty laugh in response to her gesture eliminated any of Sarah's waning doubt, replacing it with a tingling excitement.

"Uh," Debbi said, obviously trying to be diplomatic. "I—uh—think you—Mr. Craig says he knows you."

Even as she spoke, Brad had gently plucked the receptionist from his path and strutted into the office. He was as lean and powerful and thrilling as Sarah remembered. His crisp three-piece tan suit couldn't conceal his athlete's body, the bulge of his well-developed thighs, the breadth of his shoulders. His hair was dark, sun-washed, tousled. His grin was devastating. Sarah gripped the arms of her chair to keep herself from throwing herself at him.

"Well, I'll be damned," he said, that smile so wide, so frankly sexy and knowing. "Hello, mystery lady."

The secretary and the receptionist mumbled "Excuse me" and retreated.

Sarah got a tight hold on herself and leaned back in her chair, giving Brad an amused smile, which, she knew, exaggerated her dimples. "Hello, Mr. Magic."

Brad laughed and scanned the expensive furnishings of the spacious room. "So this is the office of the president of Blackstone Industries and chairman of the board of the Blackstone

Foundation." He laughed again and ran a foot over the thick carpet. "Is it real?"

"Of course, it's real!" She stuck a thumb up at the portrait behind her. "He and his wife picked it up on some nutty trip to Persia in 1890. Brad, would you mind telling me—"

"So an adventurous spirit runs in the family."

Sarah pulled her lips tightly together.

Brad sauntered up to her desk and peered at the portrait. " 'Hamilton Blackstone, 1840 to 1921,' " he read and lowered his gaze to Sarah. "Son of the guy who built my parents' place?"

"Grandson."

She watched mutely as he walked around the massive desk and sat casually on the edge—not twelve inches from her—next to the silver coffeepot Debbi Josephs delivered every morning. His eyes danced merrily. "Nervous, Sar?"

"Not in the least," she declared, leaning back further in her chair. "Have you any idea what you've just done to my reputation with my secretary and receptionist?"

"Tut-tut." He folded his arms across his chest, and Sarah could see the blunt ends of his fingers, the calluses. "*They* recognized me."

"So?"

"So indeed."

"Well, *I* didn't! Just look around you—did I lie?"

He unfolded his arms and reached toward her with one hand. She didn't pull back. His arrival had startled her, especially since she hadn't been expecting him, and their leave-taking had been characterized by their mixed feelings. But she was now strangely breathless, awaiting his touch, wanting it. Two fingers grazed each of her cheeks, pressing ever so gently against her high cheekbones, and withdrew.

"You're flustered, Sar," he told her.

That brought her around. She sat up straight, on the edge of her chair. "Of course, I'm flustered!

You storm in here as though you'd just heard the two-minute warning on a third down and goal-to-go—"

"Not bad, Sar, for a woman who doesn't know anything about football," he said, his tone accusatory yet amused.

He still didn't believe her! He was in the East 50th Street headquarters of the company; he had studied the portrait of Hamilton Blackstone. And he still doubted her! Sarah wanted to take him by the lapels and shake him, but knew it would do no good.

So she looked at him witheringly and said, "You're maddening. I never said I knew *nothing* about football. I went to several games when I was at Wellesley—Harvard games mostly."

He grinned. "Pussycat football."

She eyed him icily, but behind her cool green eyes a sensual storm was raging. "All this is beside the point. Why are you here?"

He leaned toward her, his dark, dark eyes on hers, laughing. Her mouth went dry as she remembered the moment she had first noticed those eyes, when she had sat in his mammoth bathrobe eating catnip-laden scrambled eggs. Was it only six days ago? Or an eternity, or a few seconds?

"You left me with such a tempting mystery," he said, his voice deep and low, "how could I resist?"

She laid her hands on her leather blotter, forcing them not to tremble, then fingered a paper clip. "How did you find me?" she asked.

"You suggested the phone book, remember?" he said, but something in his voice—its teasing, knowing, evasive lilt—made Sarah wonder if he was telling her everything. "Did you miss me, Sar?" he asked suddenly.

She looked up from her paper clip and saw that the laughter had gone from his eyes. He smiled and slid off the desk so that he stood near, very near, to her. "Would you believe me if I said yes?"

"Maybe." He touched her arms, then cupped her elbows in his big hands and lifted her to her feet. She didn't resist. He seemed to know she wouldn't. "Maybe not. It doesn't matter."

"And why not?"

His arms circled around her and crossed at the small of her back, then pulled her toward him. Already her breathing was ragged, shallow. "Because right now all I can think about is how much I want to kiss you, and I don't give a damn about any of your lies." He chuckled deep in his throat. "Sarah, if I don't kiss you, I think I might just shrivel up and die."

"A big lout like you?" She smiled, teasing him. "I doubt that."

He captured her smile with his lips, tasted it, brought it into himself. Sarah felt herself sinking into his arms and all thought of meetings and reports drifted away. Her denials of ever lying died in her throat. Perhaps it *didn't* matter. She wanted to laugh and fly kites and run in the sunlight.

"Did you know I'd look for you?" he whispered into her mouth.

"I wanted you to, Brad. Believe me, I wanted you to."

His eyes flashed. "That I believe."

And then they were kissing wildly, madly, with the passion and abandon of two lovers who had been apart for six years, or six hundred years. Sarah groaned at the sensual thrust of his tongue in the depths of her mouth, and answered with a sensual urgency of her own, her tongue ducking under his, circling it, tasting. The fervor of her desire, her need, made her bold. Her hands coursed up and down his strong back.

His own hands dropped down and grabbed her bottom through the expensive gray linen of her suit, drawing her against him, pressing himself and the evidence of his rising desire into her. Their kisses became even more frenzied.

"Do you suppose old Hambone would leap down out of his portrait if we decided to make love right here?" Brad said daringly, his breathing coming in ragged gasps. "God, Sar, I'd like to lock your door for a few hours and—"

But he stopped himself and drew back. Sarah took his signal and slipped out of his embrace. She tugged her suit back into place and smoothed the wrinkles.

Brad spun around, raking one hand through his hair, and cursed silently. The only thing he wanted to do right now was run away with Sarah and love her until the world ended. The feel of her lips, her slender willing body . . . But there was that damn letter from Hamilton Blackstone IV. Didn't she know about it? It had arrived the day after she'd left, too much of a coincidence for her not to know. But she didn't react to his calling the old codger in the portrait Hambone. If she knew about Ham Black, wouldn't that have tipped her off that he was on to them? *Everyone* called him Hambone!

"Damn!" He heaved a sigh and, with the desk between them now, turned back around and faced Sarah. His face had darkened, grown determined. Third down and goal to go. . . . "Okay, dammit, what's your game?"

Sarah's body was still tingling with the memory of his touch, and it took her a few moments to absorb Brad's abrupt change in mood. She stared at him in outrage and disbelief. "*My* game? Let me remind you, Mr. Magic Craig, that you're the one who barged in here!"

"You're damn right I barged in here, and do you want to know why?"

"I'd love to know why!"

He made a fist and thumped it on her desk. A very rare and expensive oak antique pear bounced. "I want to know what the hell you were doing at my folks' place in the Catskills."

Sarah groaned loudly and collapsed into her chair. "Not this again!"

"Oh, yes, this again, sweetheart." He straightened up, looking more determined than ever. "You didn't come to the Catskills just to meet me and have a little toss in the hay, am I right? Okay, then why?"

"This is unbelievable! How many times have I told you? Ten, twenty, a hundred, a thousand—"

"Don't get smart-assed with me, Sar."

She sprang out of her chair and leaped around the desk so that she could face Brad squarely. It occurred to her fleetingly, as she set her jaw and sensed her nostrils flaring in anger, that she loved arguing with him. Her hands rested arrogantly on her hips. "You big, conceited—you know why I went to the Catkills! I wanted to get away from my responsibilities here in New York and put my life back into some kind of livable order, and I wanted to check out the Blackstone cemetery. That is all!"

"Horsefeathers. I could be more to the point, but given the surroundings, I won't be crude." His eyes narrowed as he took in her squared jaw, blazing eyes, and arrogant, ready-for-anything stance. Slowly one side of his mouth turned up, then the other. "Oh, Sar, I can't wait to get to the bottom of your little mystery. But I warn you, if I don't like what I find—"

"There . . . is . . . no . . . mystery!"

He walked over and plopped down on a wing-backed chair upholstered in handworked crewel. "Oh, yes, there is," he said calmly and confidently.

Sarah groaned.

"Would you like me to tell you all I've learned about you in the past few days?"

"Please do," she said sarcastically and returned to her chair behind the desk. "You will anyway."

He ignored her sarcasm, stretching out his long legs. What he had learned had both shocked and intrigued him, and had made Sarah Blackstone—

and her brother—that much more of an enigma to him. But dammit, he wouldn't be their victim, or their plaything! If only she'd admit what she must know. . . .

"Five years ago what the papers like to refer to as the 'Blackstone tragedy' occurred," he said seriously. "Your father, Hamilton Blackstone the Third, your uncle, David Blackstone, and your fiancé, Ted Delaney, were all killed in a sailing mishap. They were adventurous men, and they went frostbite sailing despite storm warnings. Their deaths put a tremendous amount of strain on the entire Blackstone family, but particularly on you and your brother." He looked at Sarah. "Right so far?"

She nodded, tight-lipped.

"You and Hamilton were just twenty-five and thirty and probably you'd have plenty of time to learn the family business as well as follow a few of your dreams before you had to step into your father's and uncle's shoes." He leaned back against the chair, his eyes narrowed. "You're an adventurous lot, aren't you?"

Sarah waved a hand and said lightly, "Why be rich if you can't have adventures?"

Brad seemed unaffected by her feigned lightness. "And how much did your little 'adventure' in the Catskills cost?"

"The price of a Raleigh ten-speed, I suppose."

The corners of his mouth started up, and Sarah thought he was on the verge of smiling, but he inhaled sharply and crossed his ankles. "So at great sacrifice to your personal interests and whims, you and Ham took over. Ham, being more interested in the company, got to be chairman of the board and C.E.O. of Blackstone Industries. You, being more interested in the foundation, got to be president of the company—which you planned to make an honorary position as soon as possible—

and chairman of the board of the Blackstone Foundation."

"Hamilton," Sarah said absently. "No one calls my brother Ham."

"Right." His eyes rested on her for a moment, but she quickly picked up the paper clip again. "Everything went fairly smoothly for a few years, but then last year something happened. *Hamilton*"—he emphasized the full name—"quit as C.E.O., made himself honorary chairman, and left you holding the bag."

Sarah sighed. "You make Hamilton sound so uncaring."

"Wasn't he?"

"No, no, he wasn't. Hamilton expected so much of himself—"

"Not unlike his sister," Brad muttered.

She waved the paper clip, dismissing his comment. "We *all* expected so much of him. At the time of the tragedy he was working on his dissertation in cultural anthropology. Last year he decided to finish it. Who could blame him? And he didn't quit. He took a leave of absence. Corbin doesn't really expect he'll be back, but I do."

"Corbin?"

"Corbin Delaney—Ted's uncle. He's executive vice-president of Blackstone Industries."

"I see." Brad wrinkled up his face pensively. Sarah could be lying, but as far as how he felt about her, it didn't really matter to him if she was. He'd told her that, so why would she persist? She was wealthy and powerful and had only to snap her fingers to get just about anything she wanted—except him of course. She was probably just playing a game, having an adventure—with him, Brad told himself. And when he found out for sure, he'd wring both hers and Hamilton's necks and have her anyway!

But, he cautioned himself, he had to be careful. If she *didn't* know about Hambone Black, what would happen when she found out? Her family had been through far too much for him to bulldoze in with such sensitive information about what Hamilton Blackstone IV had *really* been up to for the past year. Writing his dissertation? Hah!

"So where is Ham now?" he asked idly.

Ham. Sarah bit back a smile. "I'm not sure. I haven't talked to him in a few weeks. I know he's done some research in South America."

"Great-grandad Hambone One would be proud of him, I suppose?"

This time Sarah couldn't hold back her smile, or her laugh, and they came freely, her dimples showing. How could she have ever thought she could put her life in order without him? "On the contrary," she said, "Blackstone Industries *always* came before all else with my great-grandfather. He went on his adventures only when the company was running smoothly—according to legend at least. I'm betting he had an excellent staff. How did you learn all this about me?"

He grinned. "I have my sources."

"*Newsweek* and *The Wall Street Journal*."

"Don't forget *The New York Times*," he added, laughing.

She twisted the paper clip and broke it in half. "Okay," she said, trying to stay steady. "You've learned just about all there is to know about my life these past five years. You *must* be able to see why I ended up bicycling to the Catskills—" She stopped at Brad's curt shake of the head. "You arrogant bastard," she finished calmly.

"Now, Sarah—"

Suddenly the door banged open. Sarah jumped, startled, but sighed with relief when she saw the handsome, gray-haired figure of Corbin Delaney. Right behind him was a white-faced Debbi Josephs, not sure whether to take the credit for Corbin's entrance or absolve herself of any responsibility for it.

"Sarah, I heard about the commotion down here and I wanted to be sure you were all right." Corbin's eyes wandered to Brad and took in his familiar face and tall, athletic body. "Good heavens! Bradley Craig!"

Sarah managed to mumble an introduction: "Corbin, Brad Craig—Novas quarterback. Brad, Corbin Delaney—executive vice-president of Blackstone Industries."

Corbin nodded curtly and eyed Sarah, who wondered if her lips showed signs of having kissed and been kissed.

Brad stuck out a hand, and Corbin, dumbfounded, walked two steps and took it briefly.

"Pleased to meet you, Mr. Delaney," Brad said, putting on his magic charm.

"Please excuse my intrusion," Corbin apologized, his eyes fastened not on Brad but on Sarah, as though she were to blame. His next words were abrupt and not at all apologetic. "Sarah, we've all been waiting for you."

She whirled around and read the digits of the solar clock on her desk: ten-fifteen. "Oh, damn, I'm sorry!" Fifteen minutes late. "Brad, we can continue this discussion another time. I've got a meeting." She grabbed her briefcase. Dammit, he believed who she was, so why didn't he believe why she had been in the Catskills? He had to have a reason! She smiled coolly, furious with Corbin for not retreating and giving her sixty seconds alone with Brad; furious with Brad for being so self-satisfied and mysterious. "I'll see you."

Brad smiled and cocked his head to one side. She thought he wouldn't say anything, but then he bowed slightly and said, "Right, mystery lady."

She held her chin high, strode past a speechless Corbin Delaney, and briskly asked an equally speechless Debbi Josephs to see Brad out. She did *not* want to find him sitting in her chair with his feet on her desk when she returned from her

meeting! She turned back to Brad, who was looking more amused than perplexed. His penniless
academic had turned into a corporate president,
she thought triumphantly, then cursed Corbin
silently for waxing protective when she *least*
needed it.

"Brad, I'd like to have dinner with you tonight
and . . . talk." She smiled, ignoring Corbin's
presence, and a mischievous twinkle came to her
eyes. "My five-foot-six, two hundred pound chef
will do the cooking."

She gave him her address—which she suspected
he already knew—and, delighted with herself and
feeling very smug, spun around, but not before
she saw Brad's big grin. She smiled at Corbin's
shocked face and, raising her chin, strode into
the outer office. She could handle Brad Craig!

That evening Sarah took a cab home. It was
already seven thirty, and she wanted desperately
to see Brad and convince him to let down his
guard and tell her why he still doubted her. She
wanted him to hold her, she wanted to feel that
strong body in her arms. She had thought of little
else all day! More than once Corbin or her secretary had to repeat questions to get her attention.
She had pleaded a fuzzy head from being on
vacation, but she suspected they saw through her
lie. Indeed, Sarah was convinced the minicrisis
that Corbin had presented her with at five thirty
was designed to keep one quarterback waiting.
She had made a surreptitious call to her housekeeper to keep Brad there at all costs, but he
hadn't arrived yet. Would he come? God, he had
to!

The Blackstone town house on East 56th Street
was so different from the old estate in the Catskills.
There were no fields and woods, no view of the
mountains, no herb garden, no hundreds of irises.
Sarah smiled to herself. No clothesline. There was

only the quiet elegance of a four-story brick town house in the heart of New York City. Sarah climbed up the steps and with a deep breath unlocked and pushed open the front door. If Brad was here, he was here. If not . . .

She walked through the cool foyer into the front parlor. Brad was sitting comfortably on a decidedly uncomfortable Chippendale armchair. Just seeing him knocked the wind out of her as surely as if she had been mowed down by Magic Craig on the football field. Not, she thought dryly, that quarterbacks were known for their tackling. He had exchanged his tan suit for one in cream linen. It made him seem even bigger, his dark eyes even darker, and brought out the golden highlights in his hair.

Then she saw Corbin Delaney sitting on a matching Chippendale across from Brad. Both men rose. "I'm sorry to keep you waiting," she said to Brad, then glared at Corbin, who remained expressionless.

"No problem." Brad had a delicate martini glass secured between the thumb and middle finger of one big hand. "I figured you would probably run late your first day back in the saddle. Corbin and I have been having a nice chat."

Corbin? So they were on a first-name basis now. And what had Corbin told him? Sarah's mouth became a thin, compressed line. Corbin knew everything about her, but what did she have to hide? Nothing! But she had sensed Corbin disapproved of Brad Craig—or at least the possibility that she might be involved with him. So Corbin hadn't come to tell Brad secrets about her, but to size Brad up and possibly to intimidate him into an early retreat from Sarah's life. Still, Brad didn't look as if Corbin had succeeded in intimidating him.

"Have you?" Sarah said, her icy tone meant for Corbin.

Corbin coughed a little and turned to Brad. "I should be heading home. I enjoyed talking with you, Brad."

They shook hands, and Brad grinned and said, "Likewise."

Sarah offered to see Corbin out. He demurred, but she insisted. In the foyer Corbin gently squeezed her shoulder and looked apologetic. "You have a right to be angry," he said.

"You came here to check him out, didn't you?" she asked, but the ice in her tone had melted. Corbin had come because he cared about her, and always would care. That was something Sarah didn't take lightly.

"I know, Sarah," he said, "you're thirty years old—"

"Not for another month yet."

He smiled, the corners of his steely blue eyes crinkling. "You're *almost* thirty years old, the president and acting chief executive officer of a profitable company and chairman of the board of a prestigious foundation, but tell me, how many football quarterbacks have you dated?"

Sarah shifted her weight onto one leg. "And you tell me, Corbin Delaney, how many quarterbacks have you sized up?"

He laughed. "One."

"And?"

"And Brad Craig is a charmer. He even charmed me, and I was determined to think he was more interested in the Blackstone name than in you. Sarah—" He sighed awkwardly, and his concern showed. "I know I'm meddling, Sarah, and I'm sorry. But for my own peace of mind, I had to come here tonight. You haven't had much of a personal life these past few years."

Sarah smiled and touched his arm. "It's all right, Corbin."

He shook his head, determined to continue.

"You met Brad while you were on vacation, didn't you? How?"

She told him the bare facts and no details whatsoever.

Corbin didn't ask her to elaborate. "It's been a difficult year for you, Sarah. Not many people could have juggled so many duties as efficiently as you have. I know how much you've wanted to devote your energies to the foundation, but you've filled in for Hamilton admirably."

"It won't be for much longer, Corbin," she said, not convincing even herself.

"He may never come back, Sarah," he said gravely. He looked away, as though he were sorry he had brought up the subject, and when his gaze, so steely blue and caring, again rested on Sarah, he spoke quietly and earnestly. "As I said, Sarah, you've been under a great deal of pressure this past year. I want you to know that I understand."

"Corbin, are you trying to tell me something?" Sarah asked, suddenly impatient. "Because if you are—"

He interrupted and said quickly, "Brad told me how you met—about the bicycle and the lens in the mud puddle and so forth. He can't imagine how you couldn't have recognized him, and frankly neither can I."

"Did you tell him that?"

"Well, yes, I—"

Sarah groaned.

"He asked me my opinion, and I gave it," Corbin said stiffly. "Sarah, if you had wanted to meet Brad Craig, I'm sure we could have worked something out."

"Corbin Delaney, if you think I engineered that entrance just to attract him—why, you're as bad as he is!"

"It's none of my business," he said belatedly and pecked her on the cheek. "Good night, Sarah."

"Good night!"

She slammed the door.

Seven

When Sarah returned to the living room, Brad was standing in front of a long-paned window overlooking the street. One hand held a thick ivory drape to one side, the other hand was shoved in his trouser pocket, pushing back the ends of his coat. She admired the perfect inverted triangle of his shoulders and hips, the contrast of his dark hair against the cream-colored linen, the strength and earthy sensuality and stability that seemed to emanate from his every pore.

"Well," she said, her tone the only part of her that could even begin to feign coolness, "You've got yourself another convert, but I suppose you know."

Brad turned, half smiling. "Corbin? I like him."

"So do I, the turncoat."

Brad only laughed.

Gwen Friedrich, Sarah's housekeeper, entered the parlor and announced that dinner was ready. Brad's eyes twinkled at Sarah, then at Gwen, who at age fifty was sultry and stunning and nowhere near two hundred pounds. Sarah knew she should inform Brad that he and Corbin both were wrong about her and if he didn't want to believe her, he

could leave, but instead she chuckled. They followed Gwen into the dining room.

"Quaint little place you have here, Sar," he said
dryly, gesturing broadly at the gleaming cherry
table set in china and silver.

"It all comes with the house," Sarah said cheerfully, merely stating a fact. "My great-grandfather
built it—"

Brad grinned. "Hambone One?"

Sarah had to smile at his teasing, irreverent
tone. "Hamilton Blackstone, Senior," she corrected
with a laugh. "We lived here until I was ten, but
then we moved to our . . . place in Westchester
County."

"Place?" He had noticed her hesitation. "What
the hell is it, a castle or something?"

"Well, no, not a castle, although the main house
is made of stone and we used to pretend the small
turret in the east wing was the Tower of London,
and—well, it's a beautiful place really, but not my
style." She gestured for Brad to sit in the chair
opposite her and didn't wait for him to seat her.
She had never been one for formalities. "This isn't
either particularly, but I enjoy living in the city.
Mrs. Friedrich likes to do things up."

"So it would seem."

Sarah laughed. "If it were up to me, I'd probably
have a cheese sandwich standing in front of the
refrigerator every night. When I was growing up,
my family maintained the town house, but they
used it primarily for entertaining and occasionally for overnights. I had a pajama party here one
night—can you imagine?"

His smile was rich and seductive, but she
couldn't catch his eye as he watched the flames of
the candles flicker in the crystal chandelier. "You
have quite a past, don't you?" he asked quietly.

"I suppose."

Then he was looking at her, trying to catch her
eye this time, and when at last he did, she saw

the warmth in his expression, and she sensed the gulf of experience between them would never be too great to bridge. He would never pity or envy her past or her present.

"The past has become part of who I am, Brad," she said, but sensed he already knew this. "I don't spend hours and hours wondering who and what I might have been if my father and uncle—and Ted—had lived, but occasionally all that happened overwhelms me. Not very often, but occasionally. It's been five years, Brad. The wounds have healed."

His eyes were shadows within the shadows of the candlelight. "You haven't told me about Ted," he said, not accusing her; he wanted to know more about her, he thought—everything!

"Ted Delaney was in love with someone I used to be, and I with him." Sarah fingered a silver spoon and studied the smudge of her thumbprint. "We'd known each other most of our lives, and after college we decided to get engaged. Our families were thrilled. Ted seemed to fit into my life at the time."

"Do you miss him?"

The question startled her, but then she realized it was spoken without jealousy or fear of a "wrong" answer. Brad Craig wouldn't envy a dead man, she thought. Still, she studied the spoon. Its design was simple, the silver with the inimitable burnished look caused by use and age.

"Oh, sometimes I miss what we were," she said honestly, "but the same way I miss the way I felt during my first year at Wellesley or on my first trip to Europe. I was young and innocent and free—and in love for the first time. If Ted were suddenly resurrected today, we could never just pick up where we left off. He was twenty-five when he died. When I think about him now—about his death—I feel for him what I would feel for a little brother I had loved and lost."

She picked up the spoon and felt the coolness

of the century-old silver in her hand. It seemed to connect her with her past in a small way, to all the Blackstones who had lived and loved and lost. And yet at the same time she was very aware of the earthy, strong presence of this man who had no connection with the past. It was a presence—a bond—of an entirely different sort, but equally strong, equally important.

"I don't know what Ted and I would have become," she added quietly. "It just doesn't matter."

"What does?"

She laid the spoon down and looked at Brad. His words were out of the present, not the past. The ghosts in the room, in her mind, seemed to back off at the sound of the deep timbre of his voice. He met her gaze with an expectant look. His question had not been idle.

"Sometimes I just don't know," she said simply.

"Why not?" he persisted.

"Because for the past five years my life really hasn't been my own. I don't mean to sound self-pitying, but I've had to assume responsibilities that have just forced me to put my own needs at the bottom of the heap." Her smile took on an amused, sardonic twist. "My little escapade in the Catskills was my first attempt since Hamilton flipped out to get some perspective on my responsibilities and find some kind of balance between work and play."

"Your attempt to 'recapture the spirit and innocence' of your youth," Brad quoted lightly—and decidedly unsympathetically. He wouldn't feel sorry for Sarah, and he wasn't about to let her feel sorry for herself. He raised his wineglass, as if toasting her, and teased, "Another clue to the mystery of Sarah Blackstone."

She gave him one of her penetrating looks.

He merely laughed. "So what all did your bloodhound have to say about me?"

"Corbin Delaney is not my bloodhound! He's on your side, remember?"

"Yes, but I had to win him over. *You* sent him here to feel me out. Why?" He grinned and sipped his wine. "Don't you trust me?"

"I did not send him here. He came on his own," she declared, but Brad's mouth twisted upward on one side doubtfully. Sarah sucked in her frustration with a deep breath. "Corbin is intelligent, astute, and as far as I'm concerned, priceless. God knows how Hamilton and I would have managed without him. I know he can be a bit protective of me—and Hamilton, as a matter of fact—but I respect his judgment and—"

"And what was his pronouncement on me?" Brad asked languidly. "Did I pass inspection?"

"You know perfectly well you did." She lifted her eyes to his and saw that they were laughing. She wanted to smile. "He admitted he came to 'inspect' you, if that's what you want to call it, but it wasn't my idea. He also said you're a charmer."

"And you agreed, I hope?"

Sarah gave him a long look. "You're awfully sure of yourself, aren't you?"

He laughed. "When a woman goes to the lengths you went to to meet me, I think I can be awfully sure of a few things." He thrust a basket of rolls at her. "Wouldn't want dinner to get cold, Sar."

They started the meal in silence. Sarah was fuming, but watched Brad surreptitiously, raising just her eyes for a moment, or pretending to look out the window behind him, or staring when she knew he wasn't looking. He had irritated her, but still she felt warm, eager, slightly breathless. His words and his laughter—his presence—seemed to touch her just as surely and sensually as his hands and his mouth and his body had six days ago. He was a strong, confident, compelling man—big and lithe and as comfortable here in her Manhattan dining room as he had been on the porch of the

Catskill farmhouse with a drenched, unfamiliar woman squinting at him.

"Where do you live?" she asked abruptly.

"I have a place out on Long Island," he replied. "If you'd waited a few days, you could have bicycled out there to meet me instead of up to the Catskills—which brings up another question. How did you know I'd be there?"

"I didn't!"

He shrugged. "Another clue."

Sarah snatched another roll and kept her mouth shut. Brad Craig, she thought as she buttered the roll, was the first man she had ever met who seemed to be able to stop her breath and then start it again. She wondered if she had a similar effect on him. *He's a charmer. . . .* Yes, and he thought *he* had a mystery to solve.

They ate in silence, the air thick with anticipation and questions not answered, thoughts and longing. It was as if they were going through the formalities of eating dinner and chit-chatting before they could get down to the business of touching, knowing, and loving each other. Sarah didn't give a fig about recapturing the spirit and innocence of her youth. She wanted to recapture the passion of making love with Brad beneath the apple tree!

But Gwen Friedrich entered the dining room and pointed her long, thin fingers toward the kitchen. "May I see you for a moment, Sarah?"

Something untoward was up, Sarah could tell. A call from her mother? Aunt Anna? She quickly excused herself from Brad, who automatically looked suspicious, and followed Gwen into the kitchen. "Gwen—what is it?"

The housekeeper shushed her and motioned to the back stairs. "Downstairs," she whispered. "I will look after him." She nodded toward the dining room.

Sarah opened her mouth to ask what in blazes

was going on, but Gwen urged her to get moving. With a little hiss of impatience, Sarah tiptoed lightly downstairs, where Gwen had a small apartment. She had no idea what—or whom—she would find, only that sensible Gwen Friedrich rarely resorted to such theatrics. The door shut quietly above Sarah.

When she reached the bottom of the stairs and turned the corner toward Gwen's living room, Sarah saw a familiar lanky, blond-headed figure with a square jaw, long nose, and the Blackstone pale green eyes.

"Hamilton!"

Hamilton Blackstone IV, clad simply in jeans and a sweat shirt, glared at his younger sister. He was good-looking—rather wild-looking, according to Sarah's friends, which with his perfectly natural savoir-faire made him irresistible. His hearty laugh almost rivaled Brad's. Sarah, who hadn't actually set eyes on her brother in several months, marveled at his golden tan, sinewy leanness, and glowing good health. He was in fabulous shape, but his wasn't a professional athlete's body. His year away from Blackstone Industries had done him well, she thought, and was unable to begrudge him a single minute of it.

"Is something wrong, Hamilton?" she asked, genuinely concerned.

His face was getting red as he fumed. "Who the devil are you having dinner with?" He shook his fist at the ceiling.

Already suspicious, Sarah rested back on one heel and said, "Henry the Eighth."

"Good Lord, Sarah—it's Brad Craig up there, isn't it? Don't lie to me, Sis. I *know* it is! Have you any idea what you've done to me?" he bellowed. "You went to the Catskills, didn't you? When?"

Sarah ran her tongue along the inside of her cheek. She was remembering that it was one Hamilton Blackstone IV who had told her about the old Blackstone estate and cemetery . . . and neglected to tell her about the owner's son.

"Well?" he demanded, not quite as loudly.

"Last week," she replied. "I arrived late Sunday night and stayed through Tuesday."

She was annoyed and suspicious, but Hamilton emitted a plaintive moan as if she had just confirmed his very worst fear. "Oh, Sarah!"

"You're the one who told me about the cemetery, Hamilton," she pointed out mildly, and not particularly sympathetically.

"I know, dammit!" He waved his hands at her, the fire back in his eyes. "I didn't know you'd trot your tail up there right away, for God's sake! I take it Brad was there?"

She nodded curtly.

"His parents?" When she shook her head, Hamilton moaned again. "And you told him who you were?"

"Of course, I told him who I was! But he didn't believe me."

Hamilton grimaced silently, and Sarah could see the beads of perspiration on his golden forehead. She folded her arms on her breasts and gave him a long, probing look. He looked guilty.

"Hamilton," she said casually, "is there something you should tell me?"

"No! The less you know, the better off you are." He threw up his hands in defeat. "I'm dead meat."

Sarah's face hardened. "Do you know Brad Craig?"

"No—yes. Sort of. Oh, God, Sarah, thanks to you I'm in one hell of a mess."

"Me!"

"Shhh! All we need is for that gorilla to come bounding down here. Don't *laugh!* Have you seen that man's arms?"

Her brother, she knew, was exaggerating and far more unnerved—and guilt-ridden—than fright-

ened. What had he done to Brad Craig? She bit
back her laugh. "You're almost as big as he is."

Hamilton snorted. "He outweighs me by forty
pounds. You and your damn adventures! You owe
me, sweet Sister—"

"*I* owe *you*? Look, if my trip to the Catskills is
what's caused your 'mess,' you could have avoided
it simply by telling me Bradley and Dorothy Craig
are the parents of a quarterback!"

"I know," Hamilton said, sounding contrite, "but
I couldn't tell you then. Damn, it doesn't make
any difference now. He's hot on my trail thanks to
you—"

"Hamilton, what have you done?" Sarah asked,
her brother's worry beginning to affect her. "How
do you know Brad? Why are you so afraid of him?
Come on, he's not an animal!"

Her brother was pursing his lips in thought. "I
can be out of the country in twenty-four hours."

Sarah burst out laughing.

But apparently he was perfectly serious. "Have
you told him anything about me?"

She nodded.

He groaned. "What?"

"Nearly everything. He knows about the accident,
what happened to us afterward, your leave of
absence—"

"My dissertation?"

"Yes."

"Dead meat," he muttered. "I'm dead meat."

"Hamilton, will you please *stop*? Look, if this
man is dangerous, perhaps—"

"No, no, Sarah, he's as pure and honest as the
driven snow," Hamilton said with some disgust.
"*I'm* the one who's done wrong. Will you help me?
Don't tell him you've seen me—" He stopped and
stared at his sister. "*Sarah, this is not funny!*"

She recovered and cleared her throat. "Okay,
okay, I'm sorry. I won't tell him I've seen you, but

on one condition: You tell me what you've done and where you're going."

"Uh-uh." Hamilton shook his head, adamant. "He might drag it out of you if he suspects you know. I know I'm leaving you to handle him alone, Sis, but I don't have any choice, and it's your fault anyway." He waved a hand and reassured her: "I've never known him to mash a woman."

"There's always a first time," Sarah muttered.

"Cover my tail for me, okay? I'll be in touch." He kissed her on the cheek and, with one arm across her shoulders, walked her to the stairs. "By tomorrow night I'll be safe in South America somewhere. All you need to do is go upstairs and keep Brad occupied while I slip out the back."

"Hamilton—"

She sighed, cutting herself off. What was it Corbin had said? *I think your brother might have a few shingles flapping. . . .* She smiled and hugged him. "Look, why don't you wait down here a few minutes? I'll ask Brad to leave, and we can talk."

"No! Sarah, it's not that I don't trust you, but if that gorilla gets the slightest idea I'm down here . . ." His voice trailed off, and he shuddered.

"Hamilton," Sarah began gravely, "are you and Brad enemies? I mean—"

He snorted. "Whatever gave you that idea? Brad Craig is about the best friend I have in the world, which is why he's going to break every bone in my body when he catches up with me."

"Running away isn't going to solve anything."

"It'll give him time to cool off—I hope."

Sarah wanted to ask more questions, but Gwen appeared at the top of the stairs. "Sarah, you'd better hurry!" she whispered frantically.

Sarah turned to hug her brother, but he smacked her on the rear and told her not to keep the man waiting. She hesitated, sighed, blew Hamilton a parting kiss, and raced up the stairs on her tiptoes.

She didn't get a chance to compose herself as

well as an excuse for being gone so long before rejoining Brad. He was leaning against the door between the kitchen and the dining room with that half-angry, half-teasing look on his face.

"Something wrong?" he asked, not concerned.

"Uh—no, no. Nothing." She felt like the last rat on a sinking ship. She almost said, "My brother Hamilton is sneaking out the back alley right now and thinks you're going to break every bone in his body. If you aren't, I might. Shall we get him?" Instead she swung her arms, smiled, and said, "Sherry?"

Then came a dull *thunk* from the basement. Brad frowned and arched his brows expectantly. Sarah floundered and searched her wits for an explanation. Gwen Friedrich shook her head in disgust and muttered, "That silly washing machine—always going *thunk, thunk*. Sarah, I've been telling you for weeks we must get a new one. . . ."

Waving her hands and grumbling, she started down the stairs.

Brad asked calmly, "Can I help?"

Sarah almost leaped to block the door, but Gwen, without so much as glancing around or breaking stride, replied, "No, no, I just give it a good kick and it stops."

"Give it one for me too," Sarah called down and closed the door behind Gwen. The woman was nerveless, she thought, and turned back to Brad. He hadn't moved. She clapped her hands together. "Or perhaps Scotch?" A double, she thought, no ice.

Brad's frown deepened; *now* she was lying. That *thunk* was no washing machine. Ham? He almost smiled. But of course. What had the two of them cooked up this time? His eyes narrowed on Sarah's slender, tempting form and took in the parted, soft lips inhaling quick breaths, the slightly flared nostrils of her blueblood nose, the excitement in those pale green eyes. What the hell, maybe he was just confronting the Blackstone sense of adventure. It's a damn warped sense of adventure, he thought, almost snorting aloud, and one that could get the two of them into more trouble than they'd bargained for!

He said tonelessly, "Sherry will be fine."

He turned on the balls of his feet, silently, and went back into the dining room. Sarah didn't follow at once, but took a moment to steady her pounding heart, calm her breathing, and curse her brother.

I know I'm leaving you to handle him alone, Sis, but I don't have any choice, and it's all your fault anyway. . . .

What was all her fault? And would Brad agree and blame her for whatever bugged him about Hamilton?

I've never known him to mash a woman. . . .

How did Hamilton Blackstone IV come to know Brad "Magic" Craig?

Sarah groaned in confusion, then joined Brad in the dining room. "You know, Mr. Magic," she said wryly, back in control now, "for a man I've made love to, I know very little about you."

"Oh?" He turned, crystal decanter in one hand, sherry glass in the other. His brows were raised, the scar a thick comma of doubt on that strong face. "Is that right?"

She nearly choked. That doubt again! That, she was sure now, was not *her* fault, but the fault of one Hamilton Blackstone. "Yes, that *is* right! Brad, do you honestly still believe I knew who you were when I showed up last Sunday night?"

"Just asking a question, Sar," he said, maddeningly calm.

"And I just answered it!" Her hands flew to her hips. "I'll tell you what I know about you, Brad Craig. One, you're an ex–football player. Two, you're egotistical and exasperating. Three, you're—" She paused, pursed her lips, and saw his eyes laughing at her—or with her. "You're disgustingly good-looking and charming, even if you don't believe me." She whirled around so she wouldn't have to see his reaction and added, waving her hands, "There's no dessert."

She stomped off to the living room without looking around to see if he was following. She heard nothing behind her. Maybe he would leave, she thought. It would be better that way. She still might have time to catch up with Hamilton and drag an explanation out of him.

But did she want Brad to leave? No! Never.

"Well, then," he said, his voice just inches behind her, "we'll have to make our own dessert."

That was his only warning. It was enough to make Sarah break her stride and wonder how he could have gotten so close, so quickly and so quietly, and what he might have meant. But in the next instant, before she could even begin to speculate, two iron hands were on her waist, stopping her completely.

"You're so tense," he said quietly. "Is it the *washing machine*, Sar, or is it me?" He gave a low, seductive laugh into her hair. "Relax, darling, just relax."

Gently he massaged her sides from the bottom edge of her ribs to the curve of her hips. Her conscious mind tried to rebel against the soothing probe of his fingers as they worked the tense muscles, sending signals of warmth and calm to the rest of her body. She shouldn't relax! She should elbow him in the gut and demand to know what was going on between him and Hamilton.

Yet her unconscious being wouldn't listen to any rebellious talk. It wouldn't let her be wily and inquisitive. She couldn't stop the warmth that was surging through her body, the soothing heat that emanated from his fingertips. She couldn't stop that delicious feeling of melting. She couldn't stop herself from wanting him. She didn't *want* to stop any of it.

"You still doubt me, Brad."

She had intended for her words to be brittle and accusatory, but already she was too relaxed. Brad's massaging hands crept around to her front as he slipped his arms more fully about her. She sank her head against his chest and tilted it upward so that she could see the thrust of his strong chin. He was holding her up almost completely now.

"Sarah, Sarah," he whispered in a deep, spine-tingling voice, "it just doesn't matter. God, I want you! I've wanted you every minute you were away from me, and now. . . ."

His fingertips worked across her flat stomach with such sensual expertise that Sarah moaned at the sudden explosion of heat within her. The strong steel arms enveloping her, the whisper of his breath on her hair, the motion of his fingertips—they all combined to crush the tiny, rational voice that was trying to tell her that this was a time to talk, not to love and be loved.

She smiled with delicious, uncontrollable longing. The lulling motion of Brad's large hands had relaxed her, causing her to melt against him. But as she had relaxed she had let herself open up and become receptive to the sensuous path of his hands across her stomach. Every part of her flesh, every nerve, seemed to be straining for his touch. She was acutely aware of everything within her, of her breasts longing for the feel of his callused hands against their softness. Her hands—her very fingertips—seemed to cry out with the desire to slide through the rough hairs of his chest. Her lips trembled with the need to touch and be touched.

Brad pressed his hands downward. "Don't go to sleep on me, Sar. . . ." His voice trailed off, but even his throaty words stroked her, threatened to explode the longing within her beyond her control.

Sarah lifted her hands from her sides and lightly ran her fingertips across the tops of his hands. Every hair, every bit of sinew, drew the feathery exploratory touch of her fingers. She was not satisfied. This controlled, tentative contact only heightened her awareness of him and did nothing to ease her desire to touch him.

"Brad, I'm not—"

What was she trying to say? His hands crept upward, leaving hers behind, moving up along her stomach, at first slowly, then more purposefully. He cupped her breasts, gently stroked them, and all thought of what she had meant to say vanished. She could hear his strangled moan as he tantalized her nipples and automatically, intuitively, rubbed herself against him, feeling the life of his maleness spring up against the small of her back.

She could only moan with the ecstasy of his touch, what he was doing to her and what she did to him. "Oh, Brad, Brad," she murmured. "Love me. Please love me!"

Whether he pulled her around or she flew around, Sarah couldn't be sure. But it didn't matter. She was in his arms, wrapping her own arms around his neck at last, feeling the strength of his shoulders, pressing herself against his long length.

The kiss happened before she knew who had started it, before any voices could cry out, however feebly, before she could breathe. Every dark secret of her mouth, her being, opened to him. Her tongue played dangerously against the edge of his teeth. Her fingers soaked in the feel of the masculine muscles beneath them. Her breasts strained against the fabric—her bra, blouse, suitcoat, his suitcoat, shirt, undershirt—that lay between them and the rough hairs of his chest.

Her buttocks ached exquisitely with the erotic imprint of each of his fingers.

"Sarah—God, do you *know* what you're doing to me!"

Cupping her entire bottom in his hands, he lifted her and pressed her against his thighs and hips, rubbing her against the sensual rise of his maleness. The kiss deepened. She clung to him and knew she didn't want to stop, couldn't. There were no voices being crushed now. There was only the throbbing of her desire and the feeling—conscious and unconscious—that she had never been so alive.

His mouth drew away from hers, but still she could feel the hotness of his breath. "Mrs. Friedrich?"

Mrs. Friedrich? Sarah smiled and with one finger traced a feathery, teasing line across his jaw. "She has an apartment in the basement."

The basement, the *thunk*, the washing machine . . . Hamilton Blackstone IV/Ham Black and his accursed letter, and most particularly Sarah's "coincidental" appearance on his doorstep over a week ago all flashed through Brad's mind. "Dammit, Sarah, why can't you just tell me—" He broke himself off with a deep growl before he said too much; he would have to be careful—for her sake and Ham's as well as his own—but it was damn *impossible* to think with her so near!

"Tell you *what*, Brad?"

He glanced down at her, half expecting hurt, tearful, manipulative eyes, but instead, saw eyes blazing with anger and arms folded over soft breasts, covering the pebbled tips. So he had angered her! Well, good. The determined Sarah Blackstone was back, but Brad saw no sign whatsoever of her vulnerability.

"Tell me how a woman who has her own housekeeper and eats off china and silver ends up in the Catskills drenched to the bone, half blind, and seven hours late for a supposed rendezvous with people she's never met," he said in a deep, taunting voice.

Sarah stared at him irritably, but with less disbelief than she would have before Hamilton's visit. Obviously Brad's suspicions were tied somehow to her brother, and neither intended to explain to her now. Perhaps each was afraid an explanation would force her to choose between them? Nonsense! They could work out their own damn problems and quit blaming her or thinking she had anything to do with them! *She* hadn't lied—except about the washing machine.

Brad didn't flinch under her scrutiny. Only the duskiness of his eyes and the controlled rigidity of his body told her how difficult it was for him not to touch her. *Oh, dear. Oh, damn, Brad. I want you so much, but I promised Hamilton, and he is my brother. . . .*

"Sarah, dammit," he ground out, "quit looking at me as though you'd like to run me through with the nearest—good God, is that a spear?"

She hissed in annoyance, but followed Brad's gaze to the corner next to the elegant marble fireplace, where a spear stood next to a bookcase displaying various trinkets of Hamilton Blackstone, Sr.'s numerous expeditions. "Yes," she said tartly. "My great-grandfather picked it up on one of his trips to Africa. And you're right, I wouldn't mind running you through with it! What are you going to do now?"

Brad stood back and appraised her with all the coolness of a professional athlete sizing up the opposition. Sarah wondered how she could have ever doubted his identity. He has *jock* stamped all over him, she thought, and fought back a little moan of longing when his mouth twisted sardonically. He tucked a finger under her chin. "I'm going to leave, Sar," he said softly, "and I hope to hell you know how damn hard it is for me to do anything but cart you up those walnut stairs—"

"Mahogany," she said absently, barely breathing.

He grinned broadly, sensually. "Sar, it's going to be interesting—even fun—solving the rest of your mystery."

"What *mystery*?" she shouted, and had to clamp her mouth shut before she could add that Hamilton hadn't told her a thing.

He whistled knowingly and strutted toward the foyer, but stopped long enough to glance at her and grin. "Oh, Sarah Elizabeth Blackstone, you are good." He winked. "G'night, mystery lady, and remember: I warned you."

"Dammit, Brad Craig!"

He was gone. She heard the front door shut. Her body shuddered, then turned cold. Magic Craig.

"Well," she sputtered in an attempt at humor, "his 'magic touch' extends to more than just pigskin!"

But her body was still tingling with the magic of his touch and she couldn't smile. She half expected him to burst back in and continue what they had started, what both of them had wanted. He didn't, but she understood and loved him all the more for it. How could they make love with so much unresolved between them?

Ha! They had made love when he was convinced she was a penniless academic—*or had he known who she was all along*? But of course! He had to if he and "Ham" were friends.

Sarah groaned and began pacing, her anger and frustration growing with every step across the Persian rug. Had Hamilton played Brad for a fool somehow and now Brad was simply using her to get back at him? "Poor Hamilton," she muttered with an unpitying laugh. "Poor me!"

She stomped upstairs and brought a book—the most lurid best seller she could find—into the tub with her. She had to stop thinking! But she read thirty pages and saw only Brad's teasing, sexy grin. The words on the page meant nothing, and for the first time in her life she couldn't will herself to concentrate. She looked down at her wet naked body and remembered how beautifully and sensually it had molded itself to Brad's.

I hope to hell you know how damn hard it is for me to do anything but cart you up . . .

No, she wouldn't torture herself! He was gone. But dammit, he had wanted her as desperately as she had wanted him. . . .

There was no question of that. She had seen the hunger in his eyes, felt it in his loins. Staying would have been so easy! But what would it have accomplished? Sarah asked herself. They could have satisfied their crying need for each other—had their toss in the hay—but would it have resolved anything? Perhaps Brad had shown more common sense and responsibility, understood himself and her and what they could be together more completely than she could have hoped for.

Perhaps by leaving, he had shown just how committed he was to her, to them. She recalled that sexy grin and the promise in those dark, dark eyes and felt her nipples stiffen with yearning.

She snorted and flung the book across the bathroom. "Well, aren't we virtuous?"

With another snort of frustration she sank into the hot water. She *had* to find out what Brad's mystery was and what Hamilton had done and why it was all her fault, which of course it wasn't and couldn't be. She was merely an innocent bystander. Hamilton would help—no, he was on his way to South America and no good to her at all. She would have to handle Brad on her own.

And what a delicious adventure that would be!

Nine

When Sarah returned from an all-morning meeting on Tuesday, Debbi Josephs followed her into her office and rattled off the names of the people who wanted to talk to the president of Blackstone Industries. Finally she pushed her glasses high up on her nose and said, "And Mr. Craig called." She cleared her throat and consulted her notes. "He said, and I quote, 'Tell Sar I'm playing detective today and will see her tomorrow.' "

Sarah, in true regal Blackstone fashion, politely thanked Debbi and asked her to please close the door on her way out. When the door was safely closed, Sarah counted to three before she whipped an engraved leather-bound datebook across her office. Playing detective! What was *that* supposed to mean?

Maybe he was off to South America to track down Hamilton. She laughed aloud. This entire situation was absurd! How in the name of heaven did she ever get involved? For once she was grateful for her mountains of work.

When she didn't hear from Brad that evening or all Wednesday morning, she began to wonder if he *had* gone to South America to find her brother. She wasn't worried about Hamilton; he was thirty-five years old and could take care of himself, and no matter what he'd done, Brad wouldn't break every bone in his body. She didn't think Brad was above scaring the daylights out of a deserving "friend," but he wasn't an animal. No; what worried her was what would happen when Brad discovered there was no mystery to his mystery lady after all. She had lied only about the washing machine.

Sarah sighed wearily, picking at a container of yogurt at her desk. At least the rest of the Blackstone family had no idea she had been "seeing" a football star. She had even enthusiastically lifted another spoonful of yogurt when her door opened and Brad walked in, no Debbi Josephs leaping in after him. "I snuck in while your watchdog was in the john," he said amiably and closed the door behind him. "Is this a bad time?"

"Brad!" Sarah dropped her spoon and yogurt splattered on her leather desk blotter. "I thought you were in—" She caught herself just in time. "No, this isn't a bad time, I was just having some lunch."

"And I was hoping to take you out." He ambled over to her desk and peered at the half-empty container of peach melba yogurt. "Looks like slim pickings to me, Sar. Whatever happened to the three-martini business lunch?"

Sarah fought for control of herself. She was awed by her visceral reaction to Brad, awed by the way he could weave through her life with such nonchalance, awed by the change in her—in the very atmosphere of her office—his mere presence had caused. He was dressed casually in a crisp navy twill pants and a madras shirt and had a newspaper folded in one hand, but that heady blend of earthiness and sensuality and charm seemed to permeate the air.

But then she remembered his day of detective work—and of not calling her. She leaned back in her chair and asked coolly, "Why don't you add that to your little list of mysteries?" She leveled a look at him. "Did you enjoy 'playing detective' yesterday?"

He gave her a frank, unembarrassed smile. "Immensely."

"And what did you discover?"

"That you had skinny legs when you were nineteen." He eased himself onto the edge of the desk, and Sarah's gaze automatically fixed on the bulging muscles of his thighs. "And that you didn't just attend an 'occasional' Harvard football game, you held season tickets for your four years at Wellesley. Seems to me, Sar, that you have a weakness for football that you haven't owned up to."

"For *college* football," she corrected with much more calm than she felt. How did he find out? "And that was ten years ago."

He leaned toward her. "Do you know how long I was a starting quarterback in the NFL, Sar? Eleven years. And before that I was an all-American quarterback for Michigan."

"I followed Ivy League football for four years."

"Uh-huh."

Sarah's mouth drew in a straight line. Damn the man and his doubt! Or was it Hamilton she should curse? Both of them!

"Okay, let's say you're telling the truth," he allowed. "Doesn't it still seem strange to you that a woman hooked on Ivy League football for four years wouldn't know the name of the starting quarterback for her home city's team, which also happened to win the Super Bowl just six months ago?"

"Not when that woman has been working ten- and twelve-hour days, no!"

Brad stared up at the portrait of Hambone One. Did Sarah have any idea how much her mother and aunt worried about her and wanted her to find a comfortable balance between work and play—and wanted to help? Knowing Sarah as he did, Brad figured she wouldn't want to burden them with her problems, or would simply want to deal with them herself. Well, dammit, she'd have *his* help whether she wanted it or not!

He eased himself off the desk with such grace and agility that Sarah's mouth went dry. He walked around to her side of the desk and plucked her hands up, opened out her fingers, and turned her palms upward. "I don't see any nail holes, Sar."

She snatched her hands away. "Very amusing," she said. "Now, how did you find out all this about me and my weakness for football during college?"

He remained close to her, his dark eyes laughing now, and she could see how much he was enjoying himself.

"Oh, I have my sources."

"My mother?"

She wasn't serious, but he grinned and said, "Very perceptive. We had tea together yesterday afternoon. She's a nice woman—intelligent. So's your aunt." His eyes danced merrily. "And if you ask me, Sarah, that place of theirs belongs on a mountain in Bavaria."

She swallowed hard. "You had tea with my mother and my aunt?"

"Tea and watercress sandwiches, actually," he said. "It was amusing—and informative. Did you know, Sar, with one stroke of your mighty pen you could absolve yourself of most of your responsibilities? You could make Corbin C.E.O.—he's taught you just about everything you know anyway—and cut back on your duties as president. Then you could become an active chairman of the foundation, which is what you want."

"You had tea with my mother and my aunt?" she repeated in shock. "Then they know I—about you . . . ?"

He shook his head calmly. "They don't know a thing, Sar. What do you think I did, marched up to them and announced that I'm Brad Craig and I'm falling in love with your daughter and niece

and thought it was high time we had tea together—oh, and would you happen to have some
watercress sandwiches? Give me a little credit,
Sar."

In spite of herself she started to laugh. Brad
pressed a finger to each of her dimples and, grinning victoriously, said, "You're a cutie, you know
that?"

"No one has ever called me cute." *Or a bulldog
or a banty chicken or a penniless academic.*

"So I've gathered. Willowy is more like it, huh?"
He plopped the paper he was carrying on her
blotter. It was one of New York's lesser tabloids. "I
figured you don't make a habit of reading the
tabloids, so I brought along a copy. You haven't
been getting phone calls already, have you? I didn't
tell Judith and Anna that I've been seeing their
little Sarah—"

"Then what *did* you tell them? Why would they
tell you so much about me—"

"The skinny legs I saw in a picture as we were
toddling through the East Wing," he said, chuckling. "The rest just came up in the conversation."

"But how—"

She shut up as Brad opened the paper to the
People and Faces page and pointed. Needlessly. The
faces looking up at her from the newsprint were
clear—and familiar—enough. One was of Brad in
his linen suit trotting up her front stoop. Next to
it was one of Sarah with a hand on her doorknob.
And then there was the boldface caption: "Is Novas quarterback Brad Craig trying his 'magic' on
wealthy, willowy blue blood Sarah Blackstone?"

"Oh, dear."

" 'Oh, dear' is right. If Judith and Anna get
wind of this, God only knows what they'll think of
me. They won't ever believe another word I say."

Sarah looked at him. "Lovely feeling, isn't it?
And they even have a *reason* for not believing
you. What did you tell them anyway?"

"The truth!" he declared, then added, "Just not all of it. And don't give me one of your smart-assed looks, Sarah. I've got plenty of reasons for not believing you!"

"Name just one!"

"Dammit, Sarah, will you look at those pictures?" He sighed regretfully. "And I liked your mother and aunt. If I'd seen the sleazeball who took these, I'd have relieved him of his camera."

Sarah inhaled sharply and peered at the photos. "You know, this is an outrageous invasion of privacy," she said quietly. "Do you suppose we could sue?"

Brad looked at her and wondered how often Sarah had had to deal with the predators of the world—how cautious she had to be because she was a Blackstone and worth millions. Damn, he had been so preoccupied with the kinds of tricks she could be playing on him that he had never considered if she was worried about the kinds of tricks he could be playing on her. Hell's bells, he thought; he could give two cents for all her millions! Hadn't he made that clear when he had made love to his penniless academic beneath the apple tree?

"It wouldn't do much good," he said, trying to reassure her. "I've been dealing with this sort of thing ever since I quarterbacked my first game at Michigan. It comes with the turf."

She narrowed her eyes at him and sensed he was warning her, telling her that pursuing a relationship with a football hero could garner more publicity than she had bargained for. "Brad, if you think this will scare me off, think again. I prefer to keep a low profile, but I can handle it."

Determination shone in her lively green eyes and had set her jaw. Brad grinned. "I'll just bet you can."

"Still—" She looked again at the pictures and

sighed. "My mother will have me drawn and quartered."

"She'll have us *both* drawn and quartered."

"What should we do?"

"Hope nobody in the Blackstone circle decides to pick up the tabloids today."

"Tabloids?"

He grinned. "Where there's one sleazeball, there are two."

"No!"

"Afraid so. I know it's a shocker the first time, Sarah, but after a while you develop armadillo skin. You have to. As I said, if I'd seen the sleazeballs, I'd have relieved them of their film and sent them on their way. I've done it before." He smiled cockily. "They don't usually argue."

"I'll bet," Sarah mumbled.

"Not that I have macho tendencies, but these guys can get under my skin. But I didn't see them, so now we'll both have to make the best of it." He grinned suddenly and nodded at the paper. "But what's done is done, and you have to admit there's nothing *inaccurate* there."

Sarah rolled her tongue along the inside of her mouth and cheek and studied the photos again. "Do you really think I'm willowy?"

"Mmmm."

The throatiness that mixed with the amusement in his voice made Sarah look up sharply and brought funny shivers to the base of her spine that she longed for him to kiss away. Then her secretary buzzed and when Sarah picked up the phone, blithely said that her brother was on the line. Sarah cleared her throat nervously, trying ineffectually to still the shivers herself, but accepted the call.

"I thought you were in South America," she began, one eye on Brad.

"So I'm not as big a coward as I thought," Hamilton said gruffly without apology. He lowered his voice. "I saw the papers, Sarah. You know we're both sunk now, don't you? If Brad's ego wasn't involved in the first place, it sure as hell is now."

Sarah thought of a thousand questions she wanted to ask, but Brad was watching her closely. She smiled up at him and said into the receiver, "Where are you?"

Hamilton hesitated. "New York. Look, I couldn't leave you to deal with Magic on your own—or Magic to deal with you on his own, as the case may be. 'Is Novas quarterback Brad Craig trying his "magic" on wealthy, willowy blue blood Sarah Blackstone?' "

"You talk as if it's my fault—"

"It *is* your fault, but of course, you couldn't have known what you were doing. I realize that."

Was it her imagination, or had Brad closed in on her? She realized her knuckles were white on the receiver. "We can discuss this later," she said, almost calmly. "Where can I reach you?"

Then Brad spoke. "Don't let me keep you from your work, Sarah."

He wasn't mocking her now; he truly didn't want to get in the way. She held up a hand, stopping him before he could leave. "No, no, Brad—"

"Brad!" Hamilton bellowed into her ear. "You mean he's there with you? Why the hell didn't you tell me?"

"I couldn't."

Hamilton groaned. "Is he suspicious?"

Sarah forced herself not to look at Brad and tucked a lock of hair behind her ear, very casually. "I can't tell."

"That doesn't surprise me," Hamilton said dryly, but then his voice turned calm and serious. "Sarah, listen to me. Don't interrupt. Just listen. I want to come back to Blackstone Industries. I've had my fling, you might say, and I'm ready to go back. Brad is a close friend, but he could make my return difficult and embarrassing, if not impossible. That's why I'm acting so weird, I suppose. I can't explain—I *won't* explain—but I need your help. Make sure he knows I had nothing to do with your crazy decision to go up to the Catskills, don't mention me to him—as far as you're concerned I'm in South America—and keep him away from the rest of the family. Will you do that for me, Sis?"

Hamilton was coming back to Blackstone Industries! It was all she could do to remain seated. "The first two I can try, but it's too late for the last."

"What?"

With Brad standing right there, how could Sarah explain his afternoon discussing her skinny legs with the Blackstone women? "You should get in touch with my mother, Judith Blackstone. She might be able to help you," she said cryptically. "Now I *do* have to run. Good-bye."

"Sarah!"

She hung up. Brad had circled around to her side of the desk and was looking at her expectantly, but she gave a fake little laugh and waved her fingers. "Business."

Brad's eyes narrowed suspiciously, and in that moment Sarah knew Hamilton had spoken the truth, if without a full explanation. They were both sunk. She had lied about the washing machine and she had lied about the phone call. Was Brad so paranoid about being set up that two white lies could make a conspiracy?

And what could a handsome and charming ex–football player do to make the return of Hamilton Blackstone IV to his duties as chairman of the board and C.E.O. difficult and embarrassing?

Her fake little laugh died in her throat, and she choked on her own questions and determination. How many white lies had Mr. Magic Craig told her?

She rose beside Brad and met his frown with a cool smile. What difference did a few white lies make when compared with Brad's easy, earthy sensuality and her slowly building desire to wrap herself around him? "What did you have in mind for lunch?"

"You're not going to tell me about the million things you have to do and how you're used to eating a yogurt for lunch?"

"I could," she said, unabashed, and her smile became a grin. "But I could also tell you Corbin encouraged me to take this week off as well, and I can easily delegate everything I planned to do this afternoon—"

"This afternoon?" He ran a hand over his smile. "Isn't that a rather long lunch?"

His eyes gleamed with amusement, and his mouth twisted as he held back a grin, or a laugh. Any thought Sarah might have had to find out what lay between Magic Craig and Hamilton Blackstone withered. She didn't care. Well, she amended, she did care, but she wanted simply to spend some time with Brad—*be* with him, satisfy that raw ache inside her, get to know him—far more than she wanted to pick his brains. Hamilton and his difficulties could wait . . . forever if need be. At the moment she could think only of those funny shivers in the base of her spine and how much she wanted Brad to kiss them away.

"Well . . ." She shrugged and didn't finish.

Brad laughed freely. "Suppose we have ourselves another picnic?"

"A picnic?" she asked, remembering their last picnic together. "Brad, this is New York."

"You corporate types lack imagination," he said, still laughing as he took two long strides and crooked his arm for her. "When's the last time you had a hot dog?"

Without answering, Sarah joined in his laughter,

and they walked out of the office, shutting the door and all her worries behind them.

They walked side by side in the warm June sunshine, and Sarah felt like a college student again, young and free and happy. How could she have ever thought she would feel this way without Brad at her side? She wanted to skip. She was a successful businesswoman, a top executive, but at the moment she wanted to kick off her shoes and run barefoot in the fountains. She wanted to tell all the world that she was in love with its most wonderful, fascinating male creation.

Brad looked down at her and smiled, the corners of his eyes crinkling, sharing her delight. She knew then that he, too, wanted to run barefoot in the fountains. What fun the tabloids would have with that! She chuckled at the thought.

"Where are you taking me?" she asked, stifling the laugh.

"Bloomingdale's."

"For a picnic?"

"No, you goose. I've got to send my new niece a present. What does one buy for a little girl not two weeks old?"

Sarah thought about that. "She's the first grandchild, isn't she?"

Brad slipped his strong, big hand into hers and squeezed it gently. She threw back her head and let the breeze catch the ends of her hair. She felt giddy. She smiled, aware of her dimples, and looked up at him. The sunlight danced on the gold highlights of his hair and made the scar above his brow seem whiter and thicker. Earthy, sensual, charming . . . and the man who could make her brother's return to Blackstone Industries embarrassing and difficult. *We're both sunk now, Sarah. . . .* Oh, so who cared?

"Well, then," she said, recovering, "I expect she

has everything she needs. We should get her sòmething fun and outrageous."

"We?" He laughed and pulled her close, slipping his hand out of hers and tucking it around her waist. "Mmmm," he murmured, "I'd like to *do* something fun and outrageous—"

"*Here?*"

His eyes danced with amusement, and he squeezed her tight as the lunch-hour pedestrian traffic bustled past them. The feel of her long, slender waist and the scent of her light perfume pushed from Brad's mind all thoughts of her brother and the schemes they had cooked up. He knew that had been Ham on the phone, but he didn't care. What could two wealthy Blackstones do to him? What could they want from him? He suspected this little adventure was their way of putting the past finally behind them and moving on to full, healthy lives. If being their goat would help them, why not? Of course, he *would* have his revenge.

But for now he could concentrate on nothing but how much he wanted to feel Sarah's soft, lean body beneath his. "I suppose I can contain myself for a little while," he said with a short, rich laugh.

Inundated by a sudden, dizzying wave of desire that very nearly toppled her, Sarah eased her arm around his thick, steellike waist. She could feel the imprint of each of his iron fingers in the tautness of her side. Her body longed for the intimacy of his touch, the shivers at the base of her spine coursing deep inside of her now.

When they joined the crush of people crossing yet another street, Brad's hand fell back to his side. "Darling dear," he said lightly, "if I keep touching you like that, I may drag you off to the nearest pothole!"

Sarah laughed, her arm dropping reluctantly from his waist. "Now *that* would be something for your sleazeball reporters!"

"I've learned to live my life as I please whether

or not they take notice," Brad said with a scoff. "But I suppose we'd be asking for some bad press with that, wouldn't we?"

They found more ideas than they needed at Bloomingdale's, and in one rare moment of rationality—of tearing her gaze from that granite body and those laughing eyes for just a moment—Sarah decided that no man who would shop for a new-born baby would terrorize someone, especially a friend . . . at least without good reason.

Finally they settled on little denim overalls and Novas jerseys in sizes three months, six months, one year, and eighteen months. The flustered saleswoman asked for Brad's autograph, which he gave cheerfully before jerking a thumb at Sarah and saying, "You should get hers too. She's richer than I am." Sarah kneed him in the thigh, but he merely laughed. The saleswoman clearly didn't know what to think, but she didn't ask for Sarah's autograph.

They hailed a cab and Brad gave the driver Sarah's East 56th Street address. She looked at him in confusion. "I thought we were going on a picnic."

"We are," he said smugly, and settled into the seat with her. "The other night, before Corbin came, Mrs. Friedrich let me drink my first martini on your rooftop deck. I had mentioned that it was too nice a night to stay inside, so up we went. I thought it might be a bit more private than Central Park."

Remembering their last picnic together—and how it had begun—Sarah grinned boldly up at him. "No picnic basket filled with goodies today?"

He regarded her with a faraway look in his eyes that said he was remembering as well. Finally a slow, mischievous smile crept across his face. "Some things I'm never without, Sar."

If he expected her to blush and turn away, he was disappointed. She hoped her pale green eyes matched the mischief of his. "I see," she said with regal calm.

His grin broadened so unexpectedly—so sexily—that Sarah felt the unbidden heat not of a schoolgirl's blush, but of excitement . . . and more than that, love.

With a deep, satisfied, aching breath Sarah glanced at Brad and knew that this was the man she loved, and would always love. She felt exhilarated—alive—but also somehow a little terrified.

Ten

Before going out for the afternoon, Gwen had prepared a shrimp salad that Brad found in the refrigerator and seized. "That's supper," Sarah warned.

He laughed. "Looks like lunch to me."

"I thought we were having hot dogs."

"Why have hot dogs when we can have shrimp?"

"Gwen will have your head."

"Not to worry," he said amiably. "She'd never get it off my thick jock neck."

He was teasing, and Sarah smiled. "I'm sure."

"I'll have you know, Madam Chairman," he said as he rummaged in the spice rack, "that I graduated from Michigan with honors.".

"Really?"

"Really. I have a degree in"—he clasped the pepper grinder victoriously—"communications. And, of course, I earned my M.B.A. between seasons."

Sarah folded her arms on her breasts and took advantage of the opportunity to do some teasing of her own. "You have an M.B.A.?" she asked doubtfully.

He laughed, and the pepper grinder clicked as he sprinkled the shrimp salad. "You don't think I'd turn all my money over to you corporate types to blow, do you?" He grinned and popped a shrimp into his mouth. "I blow it myself."

Sarah sighed in wonder. What would it be like to go through life with such an imperturbable rock of a man at her side? Marvelous, she thought; absolutely marvelous.

"You don't suppose there's any bread—ah-ha!" He seized a bag of French rolls from on top of the refrigerator. "Bless you, Gwen."

His good humor was infectious. Sarah laughed for no reason at all and felt again a giddy surge of love. As Brad started for the door she dug in the refrigerator and came up with a bottle of New York State rosé. He gave her a big, wide grin and said, "A woman after my own heart."

"Me or Gwen?"

He laughed knowingly, but pushed through the door and left her to guess.

The only difference between her rooftop deck and an ordinary deck, as she explained to Brad, was that she had problems with pigeons and an occasional seagull instead of ants and chipmunks. "And of course," she added, "it's four floors down to refill the ice bucket."

The deck was of solid redwood, and she had clay pots of geraniums and tomato plants, a table and chairs, and a rope hammock. Brad nodded at the hammock as he laid the bread and salad on the table. "Aren't you afraid of swinging your little tail end right over Fifty-sixth Street?"

"Not at all," Sarah replied lightly. *Little tail end . . .* "The neighbors would be horrified if I did, I'm sure. Besides, it hangs too low. If I get going too fast, I just crash into the wall."

"I hope to hell that wall's sturdy."

"Well, I admit I've never tested it." She grinned. "You're welcome to try, if you want."

He eased himself into a plastic chair. "I think I'll save my energy for other things."

Sarah noticed the sensual duskiness of his eyes and quickly sat down opposite him in an attempt to get some distance between him and herself, between the challenge and promise he presented and the temptation she felt to face them. She *was* in love with him. But should she be? Sarah asked herself. He had spent all day yesterday snooping into her background. He had had *tea* with her mother and Aunt Anna and discussed her years at Wellesley. He had her poor brother so terrified he wanted to sneak off to South America rather than face this man who was supposed to be his friend. And he didn't believe her and had got her picture in the tabloids.

If ever there was a man a woman in her position—a woman with her responsibilities—should steer clear of, it was Brad "Magic" Craig!

Not that it mattered, she thought with a happy sigh. She was still in love with him.

He poured the wine and handed her a glass. When he leaned forward, his foot grazed hers under the table. She snatched her foot away, but the damage was already done. Warm waves of passion crept up her ankles and along her shins and knees and thighs and churned in the very depths of her.

"So tell me more about this Blackstone Foundation," Brad said casually.

"What?" Sarah looked up, startled by his question. With that churning inside of her, she had expected something far more personal. She told herself she should be relieved, but she wasn't. The foundation. Why did he want to know? She took a bigger sip of her wine than she meant to.

"Well, my great-grandfather established it in 1902 in a rare fit of philanthropic zeal. He and his wife were always fascinated by archaeology, anthropology, and ancient history."

"Hence the Persian rugs and the spear," Brad put in dryly.

"That's right. The foundation was their way of contributing to and encouraging research." Sarah spoke absently, concentrating more on the virile man so close to her. Her fingers trembled on the stem of her wineglass, and she quickly placed them in her lap. They trembled there as well, not with nervousness or fear but the excitement of being with a man she so adored.

But although Brad's dark, dark eyes sparkled in the sunlight, his strong, friendly face was frowning thoughtfully.

Why did Ham want him to be a trustee? he wondered. And what did Sarah have to say about it? Did she know? Hell's bells, he couldn't believe all their sneaking around—not to mention Sarah's jaunt to the Catskills—was meant just to get him on the board of trustees of the Blackstone Foundation. All they had to do was *ask*!

He settled back in his chair. "Then the foundation supports research in those three areas?"

Sarah nodded. "Its purpose is to encourage in a broad manner the investigation, research, and discovery and the application of knowledge primarily in the areas of archaeology, anthropology—both physical and cultural—and ancient history. The foundation's methods of operation are fellowships, grants-in-aid, grants to outside agencies, scholarships, and to a limited degree, direct activities. I've always wanted to increase our visibility and expand our direct activities."

"But with Ham off flapping his wings, you haven't been able to," Brad said succinctly. He ran a very steady finger up the length of his wineglass. "Who are the trustees?"

Warm, seductive waves of longing continued to churn in her stomach, in her very depths, and Sarah had to will herself to appear cool and collected. She called on all the training and manners—the awesome list of dos and don'ts—hammered into her by her aunt and mother.

"Why," she began levelly, "didn't you ask my aunt and mother during your day of 'playing detective'?"

He grinned, undaunted. "Who says I didn't?"

"Then why ask me if you did?"

"Just making conversation."

Her pale green eyes narrowed at him. "And seeing if I'll lie?"

"Why would you lie? It's a matter of record, right?" He downed a half-inch worth of rosé. "Okay, Sar, I didn't ask them. Are you going to answer my question?"

She sat on the edge of her chair and replied briskly, "As you know, I am the chairman of the board. There are no other officers. The other trustees are Hamilton Blackstone the Fourth"—she paused after his name, but Brad said nothing—"my mother, Judith Blackstone; my aunt, Anna Hampton Blackstone; my maternal grandmother, Ruth Wellington; and Corbin Delaney."

Brad was distracted for a moment by her Blackstone manner, and he longed to scoop her up and hold her and tease her until her dimples showed, but he willed himself to ask, "Are you satisfied with that makeup?"

"No," she replied tartly, irritated with his questions—she didn't want to talk about the damn foundation!—and with his refusal to tell her he knew Hamilton. "I have always maintained that in order to increase the foundation's visibility in the community we need to invite prominent and visible members of the community to sit on the board."

Such as retired quarterbacks? Brad mused. She

was still using her blue blood tone and now giving him one of her patented penetrating looks, but he didn't give a damn. He asked thoughtfully, "Aren't Blackstones prominent members of the community?"

"We tend to keep a low profile," she said, but couldn't resist adding, "Unless we're caught socializing with famous football players."

Brad ignored her last comment. "Then what kind of people are you looking for?"

"A prominent archaeologist, anthropologist, or historian would be beneficial, but I would also like to see a person readily recognizable to the community join us."

"Such as?"

"Oh, I don't know. An author, perhaps, or an actor"—she grinned—"or maybe even a Super Bowl hero. Someone people know and admire."

Brad looked up at the clear blue sky, then back at Sarah. He was very serious. "And who has the power to bring in new members?"

"Any trustee can really," she explained. "There's no nominating committee or anything like that."

"Do you vote?"

"We never have before, but we've only taken on one new member since I've been chairman."

Brad swallowed more rosé. "Who?"

What difference does it make? "Corbin."

Brad pushed his chair back so he could prop his foot up on his knee. "So what happens if someone decides to bring on a new member and several other members object?"

"I doubt that would happen."

"But theoretically it could."

"True," she replied steadily. "If it did, I would have the final say."

"As chairman."

She smiled humbly. "It's one of my few powers. Frankly, though, I doubt any one of us would bring on someone not known and approved by the rest of the trustees in advance. We just don't work that way."

"Right."

She couldn't read his tone. "Brad," she began quietly, "do you know something I don't know?"

He grinned suddenly, the dark eyes laughing now. "Darling, I hope I know a few things you don't know."

"That's not what I meant, and you know it! Why are you asking me all these questions?" She licked her lips and tried to think of ways to get answers without jeopardizing her brother, not that he deserved her protection. If only Brad would admit everything—whatever "everything" was—and then they could go on from there. She tried to think, but only became more confused. Her brother, like his father and uncle before him, dealt almost exclusively with the company and rarely—never—interfered at the foundation. "Please tell me, Brad," she went on. "Why all the questions?"

He smiled with such sexy charm that Sarah almost forgot what she had asked. "Curiosity."

It was all she could get him to say. He served up lunch, and they relaxed and ate, discussing trivial things—what they liked about June in New York, what they hated about June in New York, the gorgeous weather, who could see them sitting on the rooftop deck eating rolls and shrimp salad and playing hooky from work. Sarah found herself giggling and eating ravenously. She chattered happily, once again relegating Hamilton to the very back of her mind. Brad seemed interested in everything she had to say. He listened.

And all the while she was aware of the steady churning of those warm waves of desire; of the deep, sensual attraction she had to Brad.

When they finished eating, Sarah went over and flopped in the hammock and laughed up at him. "It's still early," she said. "What're we going to do with the rest of the afternoon?"

With the agility—and quickness—born of two decades on the football field, Brad stole across the desk and dumped Sarah out of the hammock. She yelled in surprise, but he caught her in his arms before she tumbled headlong onto the redwood planks.

"Brad! Scare me to death, why don't you!"

But she was still laughing. He cradled her in his powerful arms effortlessly, as though she were petite instead of five nine, and grinned down at her with such playfulness and sensuality that suddenly she had to gasp for air.

"You're the one who wants to recapture the spirit and innocence of her youth," he said huskily.

She swung her arms around his neck. The feel of him—the thick neck, the taut chest, the tensed arms, one across her upper thighs, the other just below her shoulders—flooded her senses.

"I don't think anyone's ever carried me off—or even tried to." She laughed a little dizzily. "So much for the spirit of my youth."

"There's a difference between recapturing and reliving, Sarah. I hope to hell you're not trying to relive—"

"No," she interrupted sharply, then went on more gently, "No, there's never been anyone like you in my life, Brad. Never."

He murmured her name, the playfulness gone from her smile.

She brushed the fingertips of one hand along the thick, muscular cord in his neck. "You haven't answered my question, Brad."

"Haven't I?" he asked softly.

He smiled and set her back down on the deck. His look was filled with tenderness, but passion lurked behind the softness in his eyes. He stood back from her, but his touch lingered in her every pore. When he spoke, his voice was quiet, sincere.

"I want to spend the rest of the afternoon making love to you, Sarah. What I don't know about you and what you might be up to—what I may or may not suspect—doesn't make any difference to me right now. It has nothing to do with what I feel for you." He paused, his eyes locked with hers, soft and deadly serious. But I want you to be sure, Sarah. I'm being honest with you."

She nodded, tried to smile, tried to speak, but couldn't move and couldn't utter a sound. He wasn't being entirely honest, she thought. She almost laughed mirthlessly. Had she told him Hamilton had been in touch? They both had their secrets. But what didn't he know about her? What did he think she was up to? And why, why, *why* did he have to bring all that up now?

Mutely she watched him turn and walk, without a sound, back down into the house. He was leaving. Her silence wasn't an answer, only a reaction, a sign of her confusion, but he had taken it as a refusal.

No, she would not spend the afternoon with him. . . .

She shut her eyes and clenched her fists at her sides. *Not until you tell me about "Ham"! Not until you believe me!* Her mind screamed her demands over and over as she stood immobile, but never once did it dominate all that her body and soul were telling her.

Don't leave.

Had she spoken aloud? She opened her eyes. The sun was beating hot and bright on the deck. She could hear nothing but the muffled sounds of the city all around her.

"Don't leave!"

She scrambled to the door, tore it open, and leaped down the stairs. "Brad!" She raced down the hall and leaned over the banister to peer down at the floor below. "Brad, it doesn't make any difference. Please don't leave."

Nothing.

She leaped down that flight of stairs three steps

at a time and again raced down the hall. "Damn, damn, damn, I know he's gone," she muttered, then leaned over the banister and yelled, "Brad!"

Something grazed her shoulder and landed squarely on her right hip. She whirled around, into the granite wall of Brad Craig.

"Looking for me?" he asked mildly.

"Brad! I thought—I—"

The start he had given her coupled with her breakneck race through the house made breathing difficult. Now the amused twist of his mouth and the closeness of his body made breathing impossible.

He smoothed each of her shoulders with his palms, but there was nothing relaxing in his touch. "You didn't think I'd leave without an answer, did you?"

"I thought—when I didn't say anything—" She caught her breath at last. "I figured you'd taken my silence as a refusal."

"Darling," he said, chuckling, still smoothing her shoulders, "the only refusal I'd accept is one in writing, preferably in triplicate. Either that" —the smoothing motion stopped—"or a simple no."

She smiled up at him. "You're not getting either."

"So I gather."

His mouth lowered and just barely touched hers, but the invitation was there. He smiled then, close to her eyes, ever so tenderly, and let his hands fall to his sides. In one quick, lithe motion he spun around and walked down the hall to open the door of her bedroom. She followed slowly, watching him.

Just inside the doorway he turned toward her, the corners of his mouth twitching with amusement. "I figured your bedroom had to be the one with the dust ruffle and collection of arrowheads." He nodded to the glass-front bookcase of the carefully marked artifacts.

"Projectile points," she corrected, walking into his arms. "They all aren't necessarily arrowheads."

He chuckled lowly, seductively. "You missed *my* point completely—"

She groaned at his bad pun, and he threw his head back and laughed. The view of his strong neck and the roughness of his jaw forced the groan back down her throat. She placed her hand on his neck, just above the collar of his shirt, and stroked the weather-toughened skin with her thumb.

His laughter died, and he looked down at her, into her eyes. "Sarah."

He covered her hand with his, then lifted it to his mouth and pressed each of her fingers to his lips. With his other hand he gently took a few strands of her blond hair and tucked them behind her ear. Then his hand settled in the curve of her neck.

"You're beautiful, Sarah," he said quietly. "You're kind and spirited and so human. I could very easily fall in love with you." He smiled. "If I haven't already."

"Brad—"

His thumb curved up her neck, across her jaw, and over her mouth. "Don't tell me anything I don't want to hear, Sarah," he said, still speaking quietly. "Just let me love you."

"That's all I want, Brad," she breathed. "That's all."

His hand dropped from her neck, and he released her hand, letting it fall down his chest, where it settled on his hard waist just above his belt. Again she felt the churning in her stomach—and deeper.

He eased her poplin jacket off her shoulders. "You look good in green," he said matter-of-factly and laid the jacket on a trunk behind him. When he turned back to her, he was grinning. "I was just thinking of how those big green eyes of yours squinted at me out on the porch. I take it you replaced your missing lens?"

"I had an extra pair."

"Oh-ho." He tapped her chin to get her to raise it, and then started on the buttons of her blouse. His grin broadened. "How fortuitous."

This time the teasing doubt was definitely more teasing than doubtful. It doesn't matter, Sarah thought, and gave him a cocky smile. "I'm going to make you wish you'd believed me the first time around one of these days, Mr. Magic."

He unbuttoned three buttons and paused at the one in the middle of her breast. "Is that so?" He didn't seem the least bit intimidated and laughed richly. "And what will you do, Sar? Come after me with a few of your 'projectile points'?"

"Those are priceless artifacts," she informed him, laughing. "You're priceless, Brad, but you're no artifact—"

He unbuttoned the button in the middle of her breasts and slipped his hands inside her shirt, covering her breasts. Her words faded into a soft moan. Her bantering mood was clipped short, and so was his.

"There's a time to tease and a time to argue," he murmured. "And a time to love."

Her breasts felt full in his hands, but strained against the confinement of her bra and shirt. He quickly unbuttoned the remaining buttons and, with a duskiness in his eyes and a sharp, deep breath, eased the shirt off her shoulders. It fell carelessly to the floor as he swept her into his arms.

"Oh, Sarah," he breathed. "Sarah, Sarah, how I want you"

His breath was coming in deep, passion-filled gasps now, and just the thought of his arousal brought Sarah to a frenzied peak. She threw her arms around him and let her hands and fingers treasure the strength and hardness of his back.

She pulled herself against him. His hands were firm and warm on the smooth skin of her lower back.

Her lips parted, full with anticipation, and he seized them hungrily. She matched his hunger, and they kissed again and again and again—throat, chin, jaw, cheeks, eyes—until they were moist all over and panting and still unable to stop.

Then their mouths opened wide, and their tongues taunted and mingled and played, telling poignant secrets, stealing them.

Slowly Brad's hands edged up her sides until they reached her bra. His thumbs slipped inside the bands and snapped them playfully. His mouth drew away from hers.

"I don't recognize this one," he said rather breathlessly, and his thumbs slid along her smooth, sensitive skin to her back. Her shoulder blades tingled beneath his touch. "I suppose this is a business bra?"

Sarah laughed, a little raggedly. Teasing was so much a part of Brad, a part of their passion, the sexual tension that had stretched taut between them so immediately, so irrevocably.

"A bra's a bra, but—" Her throat tightened with excitement when she felt him fingering the hook-and-eye clasp. "Have you any idea what you did to me when I saw you out hanging my clothes?"

His eyes gleamed with a breath-stopping mixture of mischief and unbridled passion. "I won your heart," he said with the beginnings of a grin. "You couldn't believe a football player would hang out the wash, could you?"

"No—which is one reason I didn't believe you were the Novas' quarterback."

The bands of her bra fell loosely at her sides, freeing her breasts from the constraining filmy fabric. She gasped and tried to swallow, but hardly succeeded in breathing.

"Of course," he said, his voice more hoarse than dubious. "We'll talk about it later, darling, later."

"Mmmm. . . ."

Leaving warm, tingling flesh in their wake, his hands slid back around to her breasts, and slipped under the loosened bra, the straps now falling down her shoulders onto her upper arms. His fingertips brushed her nipples, hardening them, and he kissed her lightly on the mouth. "Now it's my turn," he whispered seductively.

He stood back and tucked his thumbs into the waistband of his pants, and Sarah knew he wanted her to unbutton his shirt. The bra fell to her elbows, and she cast it off, exposing the fullness of her breasts to his gaze. His eyes darkened, and she sensed that in that moment his breath, too, almost stopped. She could see the level of his arousal in those dark, dark eyes; in the way his chest rose and fell with deep, ragged breaths; in the thrust of maleness beneath his belt.

"I'm not sure I can," she said with a small laugh, and applied her shaking fingers to the top of a long line of buttons.

"You aren't nervous, are you, Sar?"

She glanced up at him, saw the devilish twinkle in his eyes, and knew he was teasing again. "Nerves have nothing to do with it, and you know it!"

"No?"

She refused to look at him—out of obstinacy, not anger—but continued her exasperating work on the buttons. Her fingers could only graze the hardness of his chest beneath.

"You picked this shirt on purpose just to frustrate me!"

He chuckled. "Are you suggesting I *planned* all this?"

"Yes!"

She reached the last button above his belt and, sliding her hands under his arms, just above the thumbs tucked in his waistband, grabbed the shirt and yanked it from inside his trousers.

"Whoa, there—easy." He placed his hands on her upper arms and held her still. "Maybe all your plotting and all my plotting will finally pay off."

He wore no undershirt beneath the madras, so that the firm, tanned muscles of his chest—and those dark, glistening hairs—were at last exposed to her view. Sarah smiled and ran her palms along the smooth, brown flatness of his stomach, then into the bulge of muscles of his chest, luxuriating in the thick hairs, brushing across the pebbled nipples.

"I haven't plotted," she declared breathlessly, "but perhaps I should start."

Brad growled deep in his throat, prompting Sarah's vision of him in his Novas uniform terrorizing the opposing team . . . much the way he was terrorizing poor Hamilton.

"Don't lie to me, Sarah—especially not now."

Her protest was overwhelmed—squelched—by the aching pressure inside her. How she loved him! How she wanted him! But no words came, no denial of lying, no affirmation of her love. Her passion—her need—was too great, too overpowering, and at last she could only clench those massive shoulders and press herself to him. The softness of her breasts against the hardness of his chest, she was certain, told him more than any words could.

He held her shoulders as she held his, her breasts just touching him. "I've never felt for any woman what I feel for you, Sarah Blackstone," he said starkly. "I doubt I ever will. I want you to know that."

"Oh, Brad—"

She sank her head onto his chest and felt his big, callused hands stroking the smooth skin of her back. How could she begin to express how much she loved him?

And if she tried, would he doubt her?

You're no good with words, Blackstone, she thought; *show him.* Show him how you feel.

His lips were in her hair, his thumbs pressed into the curve of her waist, his fingers spanning her back. In his touch she felt not just passion, but commitment. *I've never felt for any woman what I feel for you. . . .* He had meant what he said.

She tilted her face up toward his, and his mouth descended to her eyelids, then her lips. It was a tender kiss—sweet with possibilities.

But then his mouth opened suddenly, and his tongue, hot and insistent, plunged between her lips. The churning waves of desire flooded each of her senses. Touch, taste, smell, sight, hearing—all were dominated by the presence of this man, and her need and love for him.

His tongue snaked along the edge of her teeth, and she knew intuitively that his senses were equally absorbed and dominated by her. It was a potent thought, intoxicating.

One of Brad's long arms reached for the cover on the bed and drew it back with one swift jerk. "Flowered sheets," he murmured, smiling into her mouth. "I figured you weren't the black-satin type."

"How nouveau," she teased back, her tone mockingly haughty, belied by the way she had to gasp for air.

Not breaking apart for an instant, they fell onto the bed, landing side by side, laughing. Sarah rolled onto her back and felt the invigorating coolness of the sheets. Her laughter faded. She reached for Brad, wanting to touch him, but he growled and sprang off the bed.

"I have to wear these on the street after this," he said, unbuckling his trousers, and grinned suddenly, sensually. "Wouldn't want to give any snoopy reporters any ideas, would we? 'Magic Craig left the Blackstone town house yesterday wearing suspiciously wrinkled pants.' "

Sarah laughed, a little dizzily. "They wouldn't!"

He gave a short laugh that exuded confidence. "*That* I'd sue them for."

"Or perhaps knock in a few heads?"

"Maybe both."

She couldn't tell whether he was teasing, but rolled onto her side and, with her head propped up in one hand, watched as he pulled off his pants. He withdrew a little package from his pocket and grinned, not cockily. "All part of my plot," he said seductively, lovingly. He noticed Sarah's watchful position and chuckled. "Enjoying yourself?"

Her eyes twinkled mischievously, and yet her breath was shallow with the pressure of the ache within her, and her fingers twitched with the urge to touch him.

"Now that you're retired from football, have you ever considered taking up male stripping?" she asked, teasing him. "I know lots of women who would pay good money to see a body like yours— without the pads. Not, mind you, that I'd approve!"

He laughed, unembarrassed and unoffended. "I hope to hell there's more to me than my body!"

His pants were off, and he stood before Sarah unselfconsciously. She didn't want to—couldn't— look away. He had a magnificent body. She took in everything: the delineated muscles of his calves; the jagged scar on his left knee; the bulge of his brown thighs; the rough, dark hairs covering his legs; the tiny briefs stretched across his lean hips and thrusting maleness; the flat, hard, well-developed torso; the amused twist of his mouth; the dark, dark laughing eyes.

"Oh, yes, much more," she said, but her attempt at lightness was undermined by a dry, tight throat. "Charm, wit, stubbornness, an M.B.A. —what more could I want in a man? Oh, dear, Brad—"

He had moved toward her and stood right at the edge of the bed. "Yes?"

His voice was mild, knowing, but Sarah shook her head, unable to speak. He smiled and, taking her hands in his, sat her up. She curled her legs into a tailor squat, her knees pressing against his legs. Her hands were still in his. Slowly he touched them to the hard brown muscles of his thighs. They were exactly what Sarah so longed to touch.

She raised her eyes to his. "It's so difficult for me to explain how I feel."

"Then don't try," he said quietly. "I understand."

Breathing deeply, happily, she slipped her hands around his back, just above those slim briefs, and lay her head on the hard, smooth flatness of his stomach. His fingers ran through her hair.

The moment didn't last. The waves began to churn, and his hands slid down her back and pressed her against him. There was no mistaking the depths of his desire. She smiled and eased her hands back around to his front and tucked her fingers inside his briefs. Slowly, torturously, she pulled them down his strong legs.

She went to touch him intimately, but he grabbed her just beneath her breasts and tumbled onto the bed with her. He landed on top. His eyes were dusky, filled with passion and tenderness, not laughing.

"Ha!" he teased. "We'll see who torments whom!"

"Brad—"

He began with her throat, kissing it with feathery touches of his lips and tracing it with his tongue until every millimeter of the soft flesh was sensitized.

Sarah moaned softly. "I love your idea of tormenting. Oh, Brad, torment me some more. . . ."

"I will, darling," he said throatily, "I will."

Boldly he seized an already pebbled nipple between his teeth, then opened his mouth and accepted the fullness of her breast. Sarah's breath came in rapid gasps.

"I want you, Brad," she whispered at his dark hair. "If you only knew how much I want you!"

His reply was in the gentle tormenting of his tongue as it curled around her nipple. Then he kissed the swell of her breast, descending into the sensuous space between the two soft peaks. Slowly his lips moved lower, tasting and caressing the expanse of firm, smooth skin.

He came to the band of her skirt and stopped. His eyes rested on hers for a moment; not questioning, only promising.

Without a word he unzipped the skirt and tugged it off, not bothering with the niceties of folding it and laying it on a trunk or bureau. He tossed it on the floor. Her half-slip followed, then her shoes and stockings. Sarah lay there unmoving, wanting him, gazing at his lithe naked body. She thought she could look at him forever and never get enough of him.

His fingers rested on her hips, then caught the band of her underpants. Sarah closed her eyes not against the flow of the waves of passion churning inside her, but with it. She felt her underpants sliding down her thighs, the touch of Brad's callused hands, and then the nothingness that lay between them and their longing for each other.

She opened her eyes and saw that he was above her, straddling her without touching her. He reached for the little package and swiftly protected himself, and her. He smiled. "I don't know, Sar, but I think I ended up tormenting myself as much as you," he said thickly.

She had time only to smile back. Brad swiftly lowered himself onto her, and she arched beneath him instinctively, knowing this was right, and he thrust into her. With a shudder of passion that rocked them both, they became one and accepted their oneness.

The aching pressure inside Sarah seemed to threaten to blow her apart, but she wouldn't have exchanged that feeling for any other. She held Brad on his lean hips, stroked his firm buttocks, and exulted in his pounding thrusts.

Then her hands fell to her sides and she knew nothing but the churning inside of her, the aching pressure, and the awesome and perfect way Brad was satisfying it.

"Sarah, Sarah!"

She couldn't answer except with her body, but it was enough. For a moment she didn't breathe—he didn't breathe—and the air was silent. And then they each gasped for air, collapsed into each other, held each other. The aching pressure had vanished. The churning waves had calmed. They were lying on a quiet, sandy beach, watching the tide ebb.

Sarah ran her fingers through Brad's dark hair and whispered into it, "I love you."

She didn't know if he had heard her. It didn't matter. What they had just shared, what she had given to him and he to her, told him everything. He turned to her, and she smiled, exhausted. He smiled back, equally spent.

Much later they went up to the deck and wrapped baby presents and polished off the bottle of wine. When Sarah had started to change into her rose calico sundress, Brad offered to tie her ties but ended up peeling the dress off and drenching her in loving, erotic kisses. They made love again, heedless of anything but their all-consuming passion for each other. When Sarah put her dress back on, Brad suggested she tie her own ties.

"I haven't felt so young and free and happy in years and years—maybe never," she told him as she tied a pink bow on one of the baby presents. "Do you suppose it's your magic charm?"

He grinned down at her. "What else could it be?" he asked with a provocative wink.

"You dirty dog," she said, laughing, but she realized that when Brad was in her life, he infected her with his charm and unbridled spirit. She never once thought about her problems of balancing work and play and the extraordinary lengths she had gone to to integrate them productively into her life. With Brad around it just happened automatically.

When Gwen returned home and was about to find the shrimp salad missing, Brad tweaked Sarah's nose playfully, grinned and said, "Tell her to get used to satisfying a big appetite." Then he leaned toward her and whispered, his breath seductively hot in her ear, "You, too, sweetheart— but a different kind of appetite!"

Eleven

That evening, after Brad left, Gwen Friedrich talked Sarah out of going out to track down Hamilton on her own. "You must be patient and let the answers come to you," she said enigmatically after Sarah had told her everything.

Sarah scoffed. "I want to find Hamilton before Brad does."

"Why?"

"Because I'd like to have a go at my dear brother's neck before Brad!" Sarah sighed, frustrated. "That's not entirely true. Gwen, I'm afraid if Brad doesn't like what he finds out—about me and about Hamilton—that I may never see him again."

Gwen shook her head, supremely confident. "You worry for nothing. I can tell by your man's eyes that he will come for you, no matter what he finds. This is good, because I am getting bored making your dinners and cleaning your house. I want babies to care for."

"Gwen!"

"Look into your man's eyes," she repeated with a wave of her long, exquisite fingers and walked away.

And so Sarah stayed home and shared a can of clam chowder with her housekeeper. *Your man,* Sarah thought. What would Brad have to say about so blatantly possessive a term? No doubt he would simply laugh.

But would he laugh when he found out she had been keeping Hamilton from him?

Gwen fielded the phone calls that started about the time Sarah usually would have arrived home from work. Anna Blackstone was the first: She wanted to say she enjoyed meeting Brad Craig but was shocked at this morning's papers, and her children and their friends had cackled at the picture of Cousin Sarah and were wondering if she could get Magic Craig's autograph for them. Corbin Delaney knew Sarah had left work early, but he wanted her to know he'd just seen the papers and agreed she was willowy and knew she was wealthy, but he thought *blue blood* was "carrying it a bit far." Gwen relayed all the messages with a straight face and not one editorial comment.

It was the call from Judith Blackstone that snapped Sarah out of her lethargic mood. "Your mother," Gwen stated tonelessly, "wishes me to inform you that she likes Mr. Craig very much and she hopes you know what you're doing. She would like you to join her for lunch tomorrow after the meeting and"—the sultry housekeeper smiled wryly—"urges you to confide in her at that time."

Sarah leaped out of the Chippendale chair, star-tling Gwen. "Meeting!" she yelled. "Oh, my God—how could I have forgotten! Tomorrow the board of trustees of the Blackstone Foundation holds its summer meeting. I'm the damn chairman of the board and I just *forgot*!"

"You are too hard on yourself," Gwen told her calmly. "I imagine it is easy to forget many things when you are courting a man six foot three and two hundred and twelve pounds."

Sarah's arms fell to her sides helplessly. "How do you know how big he is?"

Gwen lifted her shoulders and said inadequately, "I watched the Super Bowl."

Sarah groaned. The foundation was where she wanted to devote her time and energy, and yet she had forgotten about the meeting. If it weren't for all her responsibilities within Blackstone Indus-tries and the mess her brother and Mr. Magic Craig were making of her life . . .

"Damn that Hamilton!"

Of course, she *knew* about the meeting. Her report had been ready since before she had left for the Catskills. The meeting was what had ulti-mately swayed her into not taking that extra week off. A reminder had crossed her desk on Monday. It was on her calendar. It was embedded in her memory for all time: The foundation's board met on the last Thursday in June every year.

She had simply not thought about it since Brad Craig had stormed into her office on Monday morning.

"Oh, Gwen," she moaned, and sat back in the chair. "What am I going to do?"

Gwen sat in the other Chippendale chair and waited patiently for Sarah to explain.

"This afternoon Brad asked me all sorts of ques-tions about the foundation: who the trustees are, whether I'm satisfied with them, what kind of new people I'm looking for, how they're brought on . . ."

"And the board happens to be meeting tomorrow," Gwen supplied, unruffled.

"Not 'happens,' " Sarah ground out, and stomped both feet on the Persian rug. "I've got to find Hamilton!"

"You must be patient."

"Gwen, that meeting is *tomorrow*!" Sarah huffed, both impatient and furious. "Gwen, Gwen, what am I going to do?"

Without a word Gwen rose and went into the dining room. She returned seconds later with the decanter of sherry and a glass, which she filled and handed to Sarah. "Drink and be patient." She glanced at her wristwatch and smiled. "Now, if you will excuse me, the Yankees are playing the Red Sox. Would you care to join me?"

Sarah shook her head, then added, "I wonder what my life would have been like if Brad Craig had been a pitcher instead of a football player."

Gwen was already on her way to the kitchen, her back to Sarah, but she chuckled and said, "You would never have met him when you did. The Yankees have been on a long road trip."

"I didn't say he had to be a Yankee pitcher," Sarah said, unable to hold back a laugh.

"Ho! I would not want to care for the babies of a *Red Sox* pitcher!"

Babies. Sarah moaned and fell back against her chair. She nearly spilled her sherry, but managed to get it into her mouth before it could hit the floor.

What had Hamilton done?

An hour later Hamilton used his key to the Blackstone town house and burst in through the front door. Sarah, on her third glass of sherry and still waiting, glanced up at her handsome brother in his khaki pants and polo shirt and decided she would be like Gwen Friedrich. She wouldn't react. She would be enigmatic.

"Come in, Hamilton," she said steadily. "You don't have to worry, Brad's not here."

Hamilton paced in front of the marble fireplace. "I know he's not here because he's out stalking me!" He licked his lips and ran his hand along his square jaw and otherwise looked nervous. "Twelve hours till the noose tightens around my neck."

Sarah calmly sipped her sherry. It was twelve hours until the meeting of the board of trustees. Hamilton stood still, peered at her glass, grimaced, and went into the dining room. He returned with a tall glass of bourbon.

"How are you, Sarah?" he asked belatedly.

"Angry, confused." In love. She gave her brother a withering look. "Brad is coming to the foundation meeting tomorrow, isn't he?"

Hamilton exhaled loudly and plopped into the other Chippendale chair. "Yes," he admitted. "I invited him—or Hamilton Blackstone the Fourth did." He held up a silencing hand, the one holding the bourbon. "Before you start ranting and raving, Sarah, will you answer just one question: Are you in love with him?"

Sarah stared at her brother, but saw that he was perfectly serious.

"Rumor has it," he continued, "you two were seen holding hands in front of Bloomingdale's this afternoon." He gulped some bourbon, then leaned forward, his elbows on his knees. He spoke quietly, intently. "Sarah, I promise I'll work things out so he won't mash you to a pulp along with me. I know I don't have much time, but I'll do it. Somehow."

Sarah sighed heavily. She didn't have to tell her brother she was in love with Brad. He knew it. "Hamilton, Brad isn't an animal. You can begin to work things out by not being afraid of him."

Hamilton leaned back and eyed his sister. "That wouldn't be smart."

"Oh, Hamilton, for God's sake, just because he's bigger than you—"

"One hell of a lot bigger than me," Hamilton amended. "And he has every right to mash my head—figuratively speaking, of course—for what I've done."

Her eyes narrowed and never left her brother as Sarah drained the last of her sherry. "So what have you done?"

"It's a long story."

"We've got all night."

There was a movement to their right, toward the foyer, then the deep timbre of Brad's voice. "On the contrary."

Sarah mumbled, "Oh, dear," and Hamilton went pale as they looked up at the tall imposing figure in the doorway.

Brad smiled and stepped into the parlor. He wore jeans and a forest-green pullover and sneakers, which made his gait silent, with a slight spring to it, cocky. His dark dark eyes rested on Sarah; she had changed into a flowing cream-colored caftan, but now she longed for the concealing folds of that massive rust-colored terry-cloth bathrobe. "Hello, Sarah," he said, his voice deep, resonant, neither doubting nor teasing.

She quickly filled her sherry glass. "Hi, have a seat. Sherry?" she said brightly, quite a bit too brightly.

"I'll stand," he said, not moving, "and no thanks to the sherry." Then he turned to Hamilton, who had adopted the stone-faced stoic pose of generations of Blackstones. "Hello, Ham."

Hamilton smiled in greeting, without showing any teeth, and gulped his bourbon.

"My brother thinks you've been out stalking him," Sarah said, as if that was the most ridiculous thing she'd heard in a long time.

Brad shrugged. "I have."

"Oh, dear."

"Sarah, will you keep quiet before you get us both into deeper trouble?" Hamilton hissed. Then he looked at Brad and said sincerely, "You have every right to be livid, Magic, but I'd like you to give me a chance to explain. I know what you've been thinking, but you're wrong."

Sarah looked at her brother and the man she loved and said lightly, "I gather you two know each other?"

"I don't know Hamilton Blackstone the Fourth," Brad said, his voice deep but losing its hardness. "I know Ham Black—Hambone, we used to call him."

Hamilton rubbed his neck. "I feel the noose getting tighter."

"You put it there," Brad said mildly and walked over to the sofa, just two feet from Hamilton. "Go ahead and explain."

Hamilton steeled himself with a huge gulp of bourbon and set the glass on an end table. "A couple of months ago I decided I wanted to—had to—return to Blackstone Industries, but I didn't want to lose all the friends I'd made in football. I thought I'd sort of ease you into the idea of my being Hamilton Blackstone as well as Ham Black. I figured you might be amused—and maybe you would have been if it weren't for Sister Sarah here."

Sarah opened her mouth to protest and question, but before she could utter a sound Brad said, "That's possible."

Hamilton looked relieved.

"Go on," Brad ordered.

"My mistake was in telling Sarah about the Blackstone cemetery—"

"Your mistake was in *not* telling me who you were a year ago," Brad corrected.

"That too." Hamilton grinned innocently. "Obviously I didn't tell my family I was Ham Black."

"That wasn't obvious to me."

Hamilton sighed. "I know that now, and I'm sorry. If I'd known Sarah was trotting her butt up to the Catskills I'd never have sent that letter—"

Sarah couldn't stand it any longer. *"What letter? And who the hell is Hambone Black?"*

Somewhere between suspicious and amused, Brad narrowed his eyes at Sarah. "On Wednesday— the day *after* you left so abruptly—I received a letter from Hamilton Blackstone the Fourth requesting my presence at a meeting of the board of trustees of the Blackstone Foundation the following Thursday, and asking me if I might consider becoming a member of the board. As you'll recall, Sarah, I hadn't heard of the Blackstone Foundation—or the Blackstones—until you turned up on my parents' doorstep at midnight the previous Sunday, and even then I thought you'd made them up."

"You turned up at *midnight*?" Hamilton bellowed. "Sarah, for God's sake, didn't Mother teach you anything?"

Hamilton's nervous chortle was cut short by a dark look from Brad. "Then that wasn't planned," he stated.

"You think I'd send my own *sister* to you at midnight?"

Brad was fighting a grin. Sarah could see it tugging at the corners of his mouth. She, however, wasn't amused.

"I had had problems with my bike and lost a contact lens—"

Hamilton howled with laughter, as much nervous laughter as anything. "Oh, Lord, no wonder you were ready to kill me, Brad! Sarah, you expected the man who played quarterback for the Super Bowl champions to believe a story like that?"

"It was the *truth*! And I didn't know he was any damn quarterback!"

"Oh, no. You mean, you said—" Hamilton gulped back something between a laugh and a moan. "You told Brad you didn't recognize him?"

"I didn't!"

Brad stretched out his long legs, crossed them at the ankles, and said calmly, "And then a day after she left, I got the letter from Hamilton Blackstone the Fourth. I was suspicious to begin with—but charmed, of course—but that did it."

"So you started thinking," Hamilton said.

"And I prowled through Sarah's cemetery and found a slew of Hamilton Blackstones, which naturally made me think of my buddy Hambone." Brad folded his hands in his lap, looking far more amused now than angry. "So I called and left a message that in essence said I suspected Ham Black and Hamilton Blackstone the Fourth were the same person."

"It said," Hamilton interrupted dryly, "that if he found out I was also Hamilton Blackstone the Fourth, I was dead meat."

Brad grinned, unabashed, and shrugged his shoulders. "I was a bit perturbed."

"A bit! Good Lord, Magic, I thought you were going to kill me—and if you didn't, *she* would!" Hamilton waved his hands at his sister.

Trying to keep her eyes on both her brother and Brad, Sarah twisted her fingers tightly together and said nothing. She remembered Gwen's advice: The answers will come.

"Ham, we've been friends for a year. You should have realized I wouldn't have really killed you."

"Just mashed me a little," Hamilton muttered.

Brad chuckled. "I still can't see 'Ham Black' as a corporate chairman and C.E.O! Look, I figured you and Sarah were playing a practical joke on me and had made up this Blackstone Industries and Foundation—so I was out for a little good-natured revenge. But then I found out my buddy Hambone the trainer really *was* this Hamilton Blackstone the Fourth—"

"Your buddy Hambone the trainer!" Sarah bellowed. So much for being a cool and enigmatic Gwen Friedrich. "What do you mean? Dammit, you two—"

Hamilton wriggled awkwardly in his seat, and Brad, feeling bad for his friend, said, "She had to find out sooner or later, Ham."

"She'll kill me," Hamilton muttered and smiled at Sarah. "I love you, Sis."

She cocked her head at her brother. Brad was smothering a grin with his palm. "Hambone the trainer?"

Hamilton nodded grimly. "Sarah, last year when I said I was taking a leave of absence to finish my dissertation—well, I lied."

"You *lied!*"

Brad, perfectly relaxed, placed his hands on his big thighs and grinned at Hamilton. "You're in for it, buddy."

"I don't blame you for being angry, Sarah. It's why I didn't tell you in the first place. It was something I had to do, just to get it out of my system—"

"What was something you had to do?"

He scratched behind his ear. "Pull a few strings so I could join the Novas as a trainer—a very minor trainer."

"Oh . . . my . . . God."

"You sound like Aunt Anna."

Brad guffawed.

Hamilton looked like he was suffering a dry throat and clammy hands. The last rat on a sinking ship, Sarah thought; she knew the feeling well.

"If you'll remember, Sarah, I've always loved football," he went on. "I played all four years at Harvard—"

"Pussycat football," Sarah mumbled.

Her brother ignored her and leaned forward in earnest. "I felt guilty enough as it was for cutting out on you and Corbin, but I knew it would only be for a year—and I'd be a better person; happier, healthier. But how could I tell anyone? I knew you wouldn't object if I went off to finish my dissertation, but to be a football trainer? If you had objected, Sarah, I'm not sure I could have gone through with it."

"So you simply didn't tell me," she said, her tone unreadable.

"I couldn't. I thought we'd both be better off if you didn't know." Hamilton's voice lowered; his pale green eyes fastened on his sister. "I'm sorry for any turmoil I've caused this year, but I'm not sorry for what I did. I *had* to do it, Sarah."

She understood. Shock and—what? Not anger, but hurt—kept her from telling him so. She hadn't minded the added responsibilities, the pressure and the work load when she thought her brother was fulfilling his dream of getting his Ph.D. in anthropology. But who was she to choose his dreams? And would she have approved twelve months ago? She didn't know. And because she didn't she couldn't blame Hamilton for not telling her. He had fulfilled a dream. Just looking at him—glowing with health, lean, tan, happy—told her the year had been worth the sacrifices they both had made.

"The letter to Brad was one way of easing him into accepting who Ham Black really was," Hamilton explained, "but it was also one way of getting you to accept what I'd been doing for the past year, Sarah. Then when the whole thing blew up in my face—dammit, I thought I'd lose you both. Sarah, take a year off. Do what you want, be what you want. I'll fill in for you."

Her eyes, distant but not cold, met his, and she said softly, "I want to become an active chairman of the foundation. If you come back to Blackstone Industries, I can."

Hamilton grinned with relief. "I'll be back."

Sarah didn't grin back. Her eyes turned to Brad, sitting on the sofa, relaxed, watching her and his buddy Ham. "You knew?" It was an accusation; they had made love that very afternoon and he had told her nothing.

Brad sat up straight, unintimidated. "Sarah, listen to me," he said seriously. "Imagine yourself in my position: a newly retired football star with a recognizable name and face, thirty-five years old, money in the bank, open to new and different options. In the last six months I've had countless offers—straight, crooked, oddball, you name it."

His pause was an invitation for Sarah to speak, but she didn't.

"Then one night—while I'm trying to escape from it all for a few days and get my head together—along comes a beautiful woman drenched to the bone and claiming she lost a contact lens in a mud puddle. She wanted to look at a bunch of headstones, and was the president and C.E.O. of a corporation I'd never heard of and chairman of the board of a foundation I'd never heard of. It turns out the estate my parents and I bought just a few months before, on the recommendation of my buddy Ham Black, is littered with dead Blackstones. Okay, fine. But then right after we make love, she decides to sneak off."

Hamilton went pale again and shrank down in his seat. "Sarah, for God's sake—"

"And the next day," Brad continued, casting a pointed look at Hamilton, "I *coincidentally* receive a letter from a Hamilton Blackstone the Fourth inviting me to a meeting of the board of the Blackstone Foundation."

Sarah glanced at her brother. "So that's why you said it was all my fault."

"Not very big of me, I realize."

Brad ignored them both. "At first I figured it was all a practical joke, but I went down to the library—just to be sure—and learned there is indeed a Blackstone family and a Blackstone empire. It was very enlightening, but damn confusing."

Hamilton reached for his glass of bourbon, but was clearly calmer now. "I guess I didn't help by disappearing. I needed some space to think. You're a good friend, Magic, and I didn't want to lose that friendship. Ham Black may not have all the syllables in my real name and none of the titles after it, but he's who I am. I haven't pretended to be someone else."

"I know that," Brad said simply, and nodded at Sarah. "She didn't help matters by lying about seeing you, but I suppose I don't blame her. That *thunk* was no washing machine."

"I told her you were going to beat me to a pulp."

Brad laughed, the corners of his eyes crinkling, the mix of earthiness and sensuality and charm there. Sarah had to fight that special, nagging ache in the pit of her stomach.

"I might yet," he said. "You duped me for an entire year, Mr. Blackstone."

"Yeah, but we had some great times, didn't we?"

Brad laughed. "We sure did."

Sarah sat very still. Her brother hadn't been finishing his dissertation in cultural anthropology; he had been out on Long Island training football players. Now he was coming back to Blackstone Industries and inviting his buddy to become a trustee of the foundation. Brad Craig, the man she loved so much that even now amid her shock and anger and hurt she wanted to hold him, had learned there was such a thing as Blackstone Industries and therefore a Sarah Blackstone last *Wednesday*. He had suspected her of all kinds of trickery. He hadn't told her—even after they had made love a few hours ago—about his friend Ham Black.

He had known everything and told her nothing.

"Will you be at the meeting tomorrow?" Hamilton was asking.

"Only if—"

But Sarah's leap to her feet stopped Brad, and before she clearly realized what she was doing, she held her head high, regally, and declared, "There will be no meeting tomorrow. I'm the chairman, and I just canceled it. Turn out the lights and lock the door on your way out. Good night, gentlemen."

She spun nimbly around and, vaguely aware that she'd had too much sherry and didn't really want to do this, marched toward the front stairs.

"No, don't," Hamilton said, not to her but to Brad. "I know my sister, Brad. Give her a chance to cool off."

Tears stung Sarah's eyes, but she kept walking. By the time she reached the bedroom and felt its darkness and silence—her solitude—she had cooled off. But it was too late. She tiptoed into the hall, but the downstairs was dark. Brad and Hamilton were gone.

Twelve

It was almost midnight Saturday, two days later. The moon was gleaming full in the sky; the stars were twinkling. Sarah had hoped for rain. She hopped off her bicycle—a spanking new Schwinn— and let it fall in the grass beneath the porch. Not a single light was shining in the old farmhouse. Good, she thought. She'd get him out of bed.

She trotted up the steps and didn't hesitate a moment before pressing the doorbell. The chime seemed to echo from within the walls of the dark house. A minute passed.

What if he wasn't here?

She shook her head and pressed the doorbell again. He was here.

Another minute passed.

The night air was warm and still, and Sarah alternated from feeling hot and cold in her navy drawstring pants and striped cotton sweater; not bicycling attire, but she hadn't bicycled far. She pressed the doorbell again, waited impatiently for fifteen seconds, and pounded on the door.

He *had* to be here!

"Dammit, Brad," she grumbled. "Answer the door!"

A shadow fell across the moonlit porch and Sarah shrieked and whirled around—right into the granite wall of Brad Craig. He was wearing only the rust-colored terry-cloth robe, which sagged open and revealed the dark hair of his chest. He grinned victoriously.

"You can hear those brakes squeal a mile off," he muttered with a low, seductive laugh.

His massive hands clenched her waist and lifted her effortlessly into his arms.

"Brad, my God—"

His mouth seized hers with such hungry desire that her breath stopped, her words crept back into her throat. Unable to stop them and not wanting to—wasn't this what she had come for? —Sarah let her arms grope for his broad shoulders. Her feet were six inches off the floor now; her spirits were even higher. The hunger of his kiss, the roughness of his jaw, the strength of his body against hers—they all felt so right.

Her lips parted, accepted the heat of his tongue,

invited it, and through the fabric of his robe she could feel his desire rising against her. He kissed her cheek, her neck.

"I was going to pretend to be a penniless academic—"

"Just be yourself," he said huskily, nibbling on the end of her ear. "That's who I'm in love with—you, Sar, just you."

He tasted her mouth again before she could speak, and she responded with all the passion and love within her. Nothing mattered—not Hamilton or the foundation or the company or her responsibilities—only this moment. Her tongue flicked into his mouth, teasing and tormenting. She was light-headed with the shock of his arrival and, more so, her longing.

"I love you, Brad," she breathed. "I love you so much! I have from the moment you put catnip in my eggs—"

"Catnip!"

She laughed deliriously. "You're wonderful. It's as though I've been waiting *years* to stumble into your life."

He gave a low, sensual growl, and in one easy motion lifted her entirely into his arms and trotted down the porch steps with her. She threw her head back and laughed at the moon.

"I ought to bring you down and toss you in the brook," he informed her.

Sarah snorted. "*I'm* the one who should be mad!"

"Ha!" He carried her past the flower bed and the herb garden; Sarah could smell the catnip and tarragon. "Have you any idea what torture you've put me through the past two days?"

"Nothing you didn't deserve, you sneak."

Her neck was snuggled into the curve of his big arm. Her body rubbed and bounced against his—starting and stopping her breath—as he strode across the lawn. She could smell his cleanness, feel the bumpy thickness of the terry-cloth robe. Her insides ached for him.

He grunted. "Corbin Delaney blames me for Hamilton returning to his senses and you leaving yours."

"I'm perfectly sane!"

Brad's laughter echoed in the still night. "If he could see you now, what do you think he'd say?"

"He'd say I'm being carried off by a big conceited ox of a football player and am loving every minute of it." She chuckled. "The brook?"

"You'd probably try to take me with you—"

"I've been practicing my tackling."

He grinned down at her, the moon catching the gleam in his eyes. "I don't doubt it."

Sarah reached up and tucked her arms around his neck, pulling herself up and kissing the rugged line of his jaw. "Want to see?"

"You can't tackle someone who's carrying you!"

"Ah-ha, but I can!"

With that she sat up in his arms and brought her mouth to his, opening it seductively and sliding just her tongue along his lips.

"Who the hell have you been practicing that move on!" he ground out.

But his arm slipped down her back, as she had anticipated, and gave her more room to maneuver. Laughing, she kicked her legs downward and, at the same time, threw her weight into her arms, which were clamped around his neck. All five feet nine inches of her was working against his torso and *should* have sent him toppling over.

Brad remained immobile and laughed.

"You're supposed to fall!"

Somehow she had ended up high—too high—in his arms, her breasts against his face, her hands clinging to the back of his robe, keeping her from falling headlong over his shoulders. He held her firmly by the buttocks. "That's what I like about you, Sar: You're completely dauntless. No fear."

He had only to shove her a few more inches and let go of her bottom and she'd be catapulting through the air. "I've got your robe, Mr. Magic," she warned. "If I go, you go!"

"How do you figure?"

His sudden move, pushing her high above his head, startled her, and she lost her grip on his robe. She hollered "Brad" and laughed.

He let go. She fell through the air, but reached out for him just as he reached out for her. As her feet were about to hit the ground, they caught each other. They were both breathing hard, laughing.

"My scrappy Sarah," Brad said huskily.

Their battle had sent his robe askew, and now it hung loosely at his shoulders, the tie dragging on the grass. She could see his long dark legs, his massive chest, and the swell of his maleness. Her laughter choked and died. "Your robe—"

"To hell with my damn robe!" He tore it off and threw it in the grass, his grin gleaming in the moonlight. "I was going to cart you up to the apple tree—but to hell with that too! Here's fine."

They were on the edge of the field, about a first down from the Blackstone cemetery. "A few of my ancestors might roll over in their graves."

He laughed and moved toward her. "Let them."

Before she could touch him, he caught the bottom of her sweater and quickly, deftly, pulled it over her head and arms.

"Did you actually bicycle all the way up here from New York?" he asked quietly, holding her by the elbows and gazing at the fullness of her breasts.

She shook her head. "I drove up with my bike and parked the car a few miles down the road."

"Good," he said and applied his steady fingers to the front clasp of her bra. "I'm glad you saved your energy."

He tossed the bra beneath a flowering almond, and, his eyes gleaming now with passion, not laughter or mischief, he traced his fingertips along her throat and collarbone, then across her breasts, touching the stiffness of her dark nipples.

"I'll never tire of looking at you," he said, "or touching you."

His fingertips brushed down her firm, smooth stomach then caught the ties of her drawstring pants and pulled. Sarah stood motionless, breathing the still, clean air, watching the man she would love forever. He tucked his thumbs into the loosened waist and slowly, lovingly drew down the pants and underpants. Crouching at her feet, he gently pulled off her sneakers. She stepped out of the pants. Her overheated feet warmed the cool dewy grass beneath them.

Brad remained crouched at her feet. His fingers coursed up her ankles and calves, sensitizing them to his touch. Sarah looked down at his dark head and the breadth of his smooth, muscled back. She longed to touch him, but he lowered his mouth to where his fingers had been. His tongue snaked out against the firm flesh of her calves, and upward to her knees.

"Brad!"

It was a cry of aching desire, a plea for more of him, all of him.

Slowly, wondrously, his mouth moved upward. His hands smoothed the curve of her thigh; his lips and tongue caressed her. Sarah's breathing grew more rapid and shallow; her pulse quickened.

Brad moaned softly as his tongue snaked across the thigh to its smooth, moist inside. With a low growl he probed deeper, arousing the very depths of her to the potency of his kisses, and his love.

When it was clear Sarah could hardly stand any longer, he kissed a hot trail to her stomach, held her by her hips, and gently lowered her to the ground. The coolness of the dew-soaked grass was a shock, but the heat of her body—and his body above her—was greater. She opened her arms for him, and he eased himself onto her, and, knowing she was ready, into her.

"I love you, Sarah."

"I love you."

And then they rocked the earth beneath them with the passion of their love. For a long time—a time that couldn't be measured by any clocks—Sarah knew nothing but her overwhelming love for Brad, felt nothing but his overwhelming love for her. Again and again her hands ran up and down his hard, sleek body, felt the deepness of his thrusts, answered them.

When at last she cried out and he cried out and the earth ceased to move beneath them, when again she noticed the stars twinkling in the heavens above and the moon shining down at them—even then she smiled at Brad and knew he would never cloy her love for him, but always satisfy it. He was just right for her. She would always need him—ache for him—and knew that he, too, would always need her, ache for her, and that this was good. It was what she wanted. She was not afraid.

She smiled at him, touched his lips with one finger, and whispered, "I'll love you always."

They eventually went to bed, but still they made love until dawn. At noon Brad scrambled out of bed and groaned. "My parents are due back from Michigan in about an hour. They'll love you, Sar, but I don't think they need to find your skivvies all over the lawn."

"Oh, dear."

Brad lent her a massive shirt, and they raced outside and gathered up their clothes, raced back inside, showered together, resisted making love yet again, and at last made themselves a huge breakfast of waffles and sausages and coffee. Sarah sat on the corner of the bench, Brad at the end of the table. Their knees touched, but neither objected. Sarah had changed into painter's pants and her I LOVE NEW YORK T-shirt. Brad wore his faded jeans and a polo shirt that stretched across his broad chest and made his muscular arms seem bigger.

"How do you find pants to fit your thighs?" she asked.

He grinned. "I don't. I have to have them taken in at the waist—about six or seven inches."

"A *normal* male—"

"Sarah."

His voice was a low warning, his eyes laughing, and Sarah giggled, undaunted, and poured syrup on her waffles. "Did you really make this syrup?"

He shrugged. "What else is a retired football player to do with himself?"

She gave him a pointed and unpitying look.

"I could be a vice-president of Blackstone Industries," he said lightly. "Vice-president of public relations and communications."

"That's an idea," Sarah said brightly. "Have you talked to Hamilton about it?"

Brad threw his napkin at her and laughed. "Why, you little snob, *he* asked *me!*"

Sarah grinned at her mistake. "Oh. Well, it didn't take him long to get back into the swing of things." She stabbed a sausage. "Why didn't you tell me about 'Hambone Black'?"

"Because I didn't think it was my place to tell you—just as you didn't think it was your place to tell me you'd talked to him," Brad explained. "From everything you, Corbin, your mother, and your aunt said, I gathered Ham's position with his family *and* the company was pretty tenuous. I didn't know how you all would react to the news of his being a trainer for a football team, Super Bowl champs or not. I didn't want to jeopardize his position just as you didn't want to jeopardize his friendship with me. We were both trying to protect him. And I've said it before, Sarah: I've always trusted you."

She laughed happily. "You and your playing detective! I was so afraid you'd find out I am exactly who I said I was from the beginning and not be satisfied."

He brushed one finger along her jaw and up to her high cheekbone. "I've never been interested in your name and titles—only you."

"Have you any idea how happy that makes me?"

"If my parents weren't on their way, Ms. Blackstone—" He cleared his throat and stuck a forkful of waffles in his mouth.

"Do Corbin and my family know about 'Ham Black'?" she asked.

"Not yet." Brad grinned mischievously. "But they will. Ham and I are doing a commercial together. He'll play my buddy Hambone, former trainer for the New York Novas, who in 'real life' is Hamilton Blackstone the Fourth, chairman of the board of a wealthy company. The ad people went wild—we saw them yesterday."

"What kind of commercial?"

Brad's grin broadened. "Beer, what else?"

"I can see my mother and Aunt Anna now! And Corbin—" Sarah shook her head and began to laugh. "It'll be good for the company's visibility, but my family will think we've both got a few screws loose with Ham doing beer commercials and me madly in love with a quarterback." Sarah held her coffee mug to her lips with two hands. "Of course, you know I'm teasing. They all think you're wonderful. How did Aunt Anna put it? 'If you let that one slip through your fingers, Sarah Blackstone, you're a fool to be sure.' Dear Aunt Anna. Now *she* would have plotted to meet you."

Brad looked at her seriously. "Sarah, do you worry about what they think?"

"Some—but not enough to make myself miserable. I've always felt responsible for them, but not because they've asked me to or even needed me to. I've always known I could put Corbin in charge

of the company and expand my role at the foun
dation, but that isn't what I wanted to do. I've
learned a lot about myself this past year. I haven'
been unhappy, only under a great deal of pressure—
but I survived."

"You *thrived*," Brad corrected. "You love you
work, don't you?"

"Yes, but it was beginning to run my life. Wher
Hamilton told me about the cemetery, I figured i
was the perfect chance to go off by myself and ge
a healthier perspective on my work. I was so dam
convinced I had to do this on my own that—well
let's just say I couldn't see the forest for the trees.
She looked at Brad, thrilled with his sensitivit
and understanding, after so short a time, of wha
made her who she was. It had to be destiny! She
smiled then, setting down her mug, and touche
his hand. "What about you, Brad? You love football
don't you?"

"Yes." He looked at her and smiled tenderly. "
turned down Ham's offer, Sarah."

"I'm not surprised."

"I'm not ready to wear a three-piece suit to wor
every day—or to leave football. It's been twent
years, Sar—my whole life actually. My dad was
college athletic director for thirty years. I wouldn'
be happy in a corporation, but I would like to be
trustee of the foundation." He grinned. "Unless
you veto me."

Sarah scoffed. "And pay the consequences?"

"I'd tackle you the first chance I got," he said
his eyes twinkling.

"Mmmm, I might veto you after all."

He laughed, but then went on seriously. "I've
decided to accept a network offer to do announcing
I think it'll be fun—and challenging. I haven'
watched a whole lot of football, but I know th
game pretty well."

"I would say that's an understatement." Sarah
pursed her lips, mischief in her eyes, her dimple

two dots of amusement. "Does this mean I'll have to start reading the sports pages? I wouldn't want to mistake one six-foot-three two-hundred-twelve-pound meat for *my* six-foot-three two-hundred-twelve-pound meat—"

He nearly sprang out of his chair. "How did you know my height and weight, Sarah Blackstone, if you'd never heard of me!"

"Gwen Friedrich."

"I should have known." He gave a short laugh. "She's on my side, I hope? If I'm going to be living with the woman—"

"Brad! You mean, you'll live in the town house?"

"Do you think I'd steal you away from your projectile points? Besides, I'm partial to that rooftop deck of yours. But if Gwen doesn't approve of me—"

"You don't have to worry," Sarah said, not that he was. "She adores you. She calls you my man."

Brad threw his head back and laughed heartily. Swallowing a grin, Sarah made a fist—a proper fist, as he had taught her—and straightening her arm, lay back and belted him in his rock-hard gut.

His hand clamped down on her wrist, jerking her off the bench and onto his lap. "What did I tell you about taking on someone bigger than you, scrappy?" His breath was hot in her face, his dark, dark eyes glistening, passion lurking just behind them. "You didn't run fast enough."

She grinned up at him. "I didn't want to run."

"You couldn't run fast enough, sweetheart," he murmured. "I'd be after you—"

His mouth descended toward hers, but the sound of a car in the driveway stopped them. "Your parents!" Sarah leaped off Brad's lap and started clearing the dishes. Brad wasn't far behind.

"They've been gone two weeks, and I've met and fallen in love with the woman I want to marry. . . ."

His voice trailed off. Sarah looked at him, empty

waffle plate in hand, her eyes filled with love. "We can have the ceremony out here," she said breathlessly. "This fall, just when the leaves have turned. Oh, Brad, it'll be lovely!"

He grinned at her. "Yes," he said thickly, "it will."

"Brad?" came the strong voice of an older woman, the shutting of the front door, footsteps. "Do you realize there's a Rolls-Royce parked just down the road? It's the strangest thing! Not a soul in sight—"

Brad glanced down at Sarah. "A Rolls?"

She shrugged. "I don't have a car, so I had to borrow my mother's."

He chuckled, a deep, sensuous sound that rolled from his throat.

His parents appeared in the doorway. Dorothy Craig stood two inches taller than Sarah, and Brad had her dark, dark eyes and tousled hair, though hers had wisps of gray in it. She wore a summery yellow cotton dress. Bradley Craig, Sr., was as tall as his son and had his strong, friendly face, but not much hair. He wore khaki pants and a pullover. They had the glow of two new grandparents.

Dorothy Craig's eyes fell on Sarah. "Oh, excuse me."

"No, no, Mother," Brad said, laughing. "It's all right. Mother, Father, I'd like you to meet Sarah Blackstone. Sarah, my parents, Bradley and Dorothy Craig."

"Sarah Blackstone!" the senior Craig said in a voice as deep as his son's. "It's good to meet you at last, Sarah. Did you just arrive? Have you seen the cemetery yet?"

Dorothy Craig beamed. "I'm so glad you made arrangements with Brad to come. I'm sorry we had to delay your trip, but you know you can't tell a baby when to be born." She laughed. "Do let me show you around. Bradley and I have researched the house and can show you what was part of the original structure and what has been added later—"

"Mother," Brad said, and took Sarah's hand. "Maybe you and Father should sit down and have a cup of coffee."

"I'm so pleased to meet you," Sarah said, smiling and thinking of what her Aunt Anna would say. This sort of thing, she knew, wasn't covered in Emily Post. "Brad has been very accommodating."

He cut short a laugh and pulled out a chair at the table. "Sit down," he offered. "We have quite a story to tell."

His mother sat down. "Oh?"

His father poured the coffee. "This wouldn't have anything to do with the Rolls parked down the road and the bicycle on the front lawn, would it?"

"Well . . ."

Brad and Sarah waited until the couple were seated before they sat on the bench together and began their story.

"You remember my friend Ham Black?" Brad asked.

They said they did. "He was the one who told you about this place," Dorothy Craig said.

"Right."

"He's my brother," Sarah said. "Hamilton Blackstone the Fourth, chairman of the board and chief executive officer of Blackstone Industries."

Brad nodded. "Only I didn't know that until last week."

Sarah got up and put on another pot of coffee, not taking her eyes off Brad for more than a few seconds. She sensed his mother watching her and met her eyes briefly, but in that moment Sarah knew she had told the older woman all she needed to know: The woman who had come to look at the gravestones of her ancestors was very deeply in love with Brad Craig, and always would be.

THE EDITOR'S CORNER

Ti amo. Ich liebe dich. Je t'aime. I love you. Those words along with all the other magical words in our LOVESWEPT romances are read by women around the world. We thought you'd be interested to learn that our books are translated into lots of languages for publication in many, many countries. So you share our delicious stories with women everywhere: Australia, Germany, France, New Zealand, Sweden, Norway, the Philippines . . . I could go on and on. And fan mail reaches us with the most exotic postmarks—Selangor, Malaysia, for example. Those postmarks certainly conjure romantic images for us on the LOVESWEPT staff. It is deeply touching to know that the tenderness, humor, warmth, sensuality—all the elements of loving in our LOVESWEPT romances—are enjoyed equally by the reader in Kansas City and in Kuala Lumpur. Close your eyes. Can you imagine the globe circled by women touching hands, sharing the common belief that stories about loving relationships are the best entertainment of all? It's a beautiful image, isn't it?

Now from the universal to the particular—namely, the treats in store for you next month.

Heading off the April LOVESWEPT list is Joan Domning's fourth romance, **KIRSTEN'S INHERITANCE,** LOVESWEPT #29. This absolutely heartwarming story is set in the tiny town of Avlum, Minnesota, and features the colorful and sexy hero, Dr. Cory Antonelli. The darling doctor rocks the town Kirsten has grown up in. (His jogging clothes appear to be underwear to the small town folks amazed by his activities in their midst.) And he is so darkly handsome in a town of fair people of Scandinavian heritage that not a single thing he does can escape notice. Author Joan knows of what she speaks! She was born and raised in a community

(continued)

quite similar to the imaginary one in which she sets this charming book. There are creative twists galore in this love story that I feel sure you're going to add to your collection of "keepers."

OOO-h, that Iris Johansen! Better read **RETURN TO SANTA FLORES,** LOVESWEPT #40, with great care! It's always a challenge to try to figure out which of Iris's secondary characters has his or her own love story next, isn't it? One hint: maybe the way to a woman's heart is *not* via the palate, but another sense. Now, though, let's focus on the marvelous romance between Steve and Jenny in **RETURN TO SANTA FLORES.** First, you'll notice that the opening chapter takes place eight years before chapter two. It's almost a prologue to the story and a delightful innovation in the writing craft for this particular romance. Steve considers himself years too old and jaded for Jenny . . . but she won't take "no" for an answer. Her scrapes and Steve's last minute rescues become legendary around the hotel he owns, but through everything the real question still remains: can Steve resist Jenny's love? There is a comic scene in a motel bedroom in this, Iris's eighth romance, that is priceless!

What a pleasure to be able to introduce yet another talented newcomer as a LOVESWEPT author. **THE SOPHISTICATED MOUNTAIN GAL,** LOVESWEPT #41, is Joan Bramsch's first novel. And it's a "WOW" of a love story. Crissy Brant is one of the most vivacious and wide-ranging heroines we've published. She is an Ozark Mountain gal, but she's also a sophisticated and well-trained actress with a unique ability to create characters in many different voices. James Prince, a disillusioned ad man recently transplanted to Bransom, Missouri, has started a new life as a toy manufacturer. He falls in love first with Crissy in her role of Tulip Bloom, the Silver Dollar City storyteller . . . and soon he's in love with all the other Crissy Brants, too. But outsiders don't win trust easily and James has several strikes against him—so the path to true love for these two delightful characters is as hard to negotiate as a steep and stone-strewn mountain road. By the way, there is a twenty-plus page "temptation" scene in this book that I guarantee will knock your socks off! My, oh my! Welcome to LOVESWEPT, Joan Bramsch!

Sara Orwig's first LOVESWEPT, **AUTUMN FLAMES,** received wonderful fan mail! Now Sara's topped even that romance with **HEAT WAVE,** LOVESWEPT #42. Marilee O'Neil literally drops into Cole Chandler's lap. Imagine Cole's surprise when, while sunbathing nude, a hot air balloon piloted by Marilee plunks down in the middle of his swimming pool. She claims to lead a dull and ordinary life—and perhaps that was the case *before* she met Cole. But life is anything but ordinary around this extraordinary hero. From painting his house on his wheat farm, to tutoring his nephew, to single-handedly capturing two rustlers on his property, Marilee's existence simmers in Cole's company. It's the hottest summer Kansas has known in recorded history ... but the weather is cool in comparison to the sizzling love affair between two touching human beings. Sara Orwig just gets better and better all the time!

It's a pleasure to work with all these fine LOVESWEPT authors and a pleasure to hear from you that you are enjoying the series so much!

Until next month, we send warmest good wishes,

Sincerely,

Carolyn Nichols

Carolyn Nichols
  Editor
LOVESWEPT
Bantam Books, Inc.
666 Fifth Avenue
New York, NY 10103

LOVESWEPT

Love Stories you'll never forget by authors you'll always remember

☐	21603	**Heaven's Price #1** Sandra Brown	$1.95
☐	21604	**Surrender #2** Helen Mittermeyer	$1.95
☐	21600	**The Joining Stone #3** Noelle Berry McCue	$1.95
☐	21601	**Silver Miracles #4** Fayrene Preston	$1.95
☐	21605	**Matching Wits #5** Carla Neggers	$1.95
☐	21606	**A Love for All Time #6** Dorothy Garlock	$1.95
☐	21607	**A Tryst With Mr. Lincoln? #7** Billie Green	$1.95
☐	21602	**Temptation's Sting #8** Helen Conrad	$1.95
☐	21608	**December 32nd . . . And Always #9** Marie Michael	$1.95
☐	21609	**Hard Drivin' Man #10** Nancy Carlson	$1.95
☐	21610	**Beloved Intruder #11** Noelle Berry McCue	$1.95
☐	21611	**Hunter's Payne #12** Joan J. Domning	$1.95
☐	21618	**Tiger Lady #13** Joan Domning	$1.95
☐	21613	**Stormy Vows #14** Iris Johansen	$1.95
☐	21614	**Brief Delight #15** Helen Mittermeyer	$1.95
☐	21616	**A Very Reluctant Knight #16** Billie Green	$1.95
☐	21617	**Tempest at Sea #17** Iris Johansen	$1.95
☐	21619	**Autumn Flames #18** Sara Orwig	$1.95
☐	21620	**Pfarr Lake Affair #19** Joan Domning	$1.95
☐	21621	**Heart on a String #20** Carla Neggars	$1.95
☐	21622	**The Seduction of Jason #21** Fayrene Preston	$1.95
☐	21623	**Breakfast In Bed #22** Sandra Brown	$1.95
☐	21624	**Taking Savannah #23** Becky Combs	$1.95
☐	21625	**The Reluctant Lark #24** Iris Johansen	$1.95

Prices and availability subject to change without notice.

Buy them at your local bookstore or use this handy coupon for ordering:

Bantam Books, Inc., Dept. SW, 414 East Golf Road, Des Plaines, Ill. 60016

Please send me the books I have checked above. I am enclosing $_____ (please add $1.25 to cover postage and handling). Send check or money order—no cash or C.O.D.'s please.

Mr/Ms_____

Address _____

City/State_____ Zip_____

SW—3/84

Please allow four to six weeks for delivery. This offer expires 9/84.

LOVESWEPT

Love Stories you'll never forget by authors you'll always remember